UNDER THE EAGLE'S WINGS

Sam Everett, owner of Everett Wings Charter Jet Service, represents everything to which Codie Merideth is opposed — wealth, worldliness and self-indulgence. When Sam tries to draw Codie into his world, she sets her heels against it, afraid that, once there, she would never be able to follow her dream of building a haven for homeless children. Only when Sam and Codie nearly lose their lives in Sam's plane, does Codie realize just how much life has to offer.

AU

BETTY W. KINSER

UNDER THE EAGLE'S WINGS

Complete and Unabridged

LINFORD
Leicester

First published in Great Britain in 1991 by
Robert Hale Limited
London

First Linford Edition
published 1998
by arrangement with
Robert Hale Limited
London

British Library CIP Data

Kinser, Betty W.
    Under the eagle's wings.—Large print ed.—
Linford romance library
    1. Love stories
    2. Large type books
    I. Title
    823.9'14 [F]

    ISBN 0–7089–5235–6

Published by
F. A. Thorpe (Publishing) Ltd.
Anstey, Leicestershire

Set by Words & Graphics Ltd.
Anstey, Leicestershire
Printed and bound in Great Britain by
T. J. International Ltd., Padstow, Cornwall

This book is printed on acid-free paper

1

CODIE MERIDETH sat for awhile at the tiny formica table, staring with little interest at the dirty dishes stacked there. She and her sister Marlena had finished a late supper and Marlena (claiming an early morning photo session) had gone straight to bed.

Codie knew she spoiled Marlena. After their parents had died in a boating accident, Codie had become, at the age of fifteen, both mother and father to Marlena, vowing to protect her sister from whatever pain and unhappiness she could. At times, it was an awesome burden.

Piling the dishes in the sink, she turned on the tap and watched the stream of tepid water trickle out. In the year she and Marlena had lived in their scantily furnished one-bedroom apartment, Codie had pleaded with the landlord at least a dozen times to fix the hot water heater, but all she got for her efforts were promises of no apparent value.

She ran her fingers through her short-cropped auburn hair and slumped toward the sink with a sigh of defeat. What could she expect from a landlord who charged so little?

A year ago Codie Merideth had just begun her job as Youth Director for Rock Creek Community Center — the first female director in its history — when she had received an urgent call from Marlena.

"You have to come to the city, Codie!" Marlena had insisted. "This is my big chance."

So Codie had traded the tree-covered hills of the Ozarks for city life; giving up her passionate dream of some day building a home for children who needed special love. While Marlena took advantage of her 'big chance' to become a top-notch photographer's model with the prestigious Bev Sloan Agency, Codie worked to support the two of them.

Codie shook her head to clear it of her daydreaming, and set about picking up Marlena's clutter that was strewn over the small living room. At last, tasks aside, Codie curled up in a corner of the sofa and opened a book, hoping to read until she felt sleepy.

The jangling of the telephone startled her. She twisted around and picked up the receiver, her neatly arched eyebrows drawn together in disapproval that anyone should phone at such a late hour.

"Hello?"

"Miss Merideth?"

"Yes, this is Codie Merideth."

"No . . . I'm calling for Marlena. Is she there?"

Codie glanced toward the closed bedroom door and decided against disturbing her sister, no matter who the caller.

"Yes, she is, but she can't come to

the phone. She's gone to bed."

"Well, wake her up. I need to talk to her right away."

Codie forced cool politeness into her voice.

"I'm sorry, but I won't do that. Can't this wait until in the morning?"

"Who did you say you are?" The man's voice was as smooth and clear as Ozark mountain water. Even in his rudeness, his voice carried a warm, musical quality.

"I'm Codie Merideth, Marlena's sister." Not that it's any of your business, she wanted to add.

"Well, Miss Codie Merideth, I'm Sam Everett and your sister was supposed to meet me at eight o'clock for a re-take on some photos."

"I repeat . . . can't this wait until morning?"

"No! It's already waited too long. If she wants to work for me, she is going to have to learn better discipline. This is the third time she has failed to show up for a session."

4

"I see. Are you with the Sloan Agency?"

"No. I'm the man who owns the company for which she seems uninterested in doing any modelling."

Codie braced the phone against one straight, square shoulder and tucked her stockinged feet beneath her. Facts swiftly flew across her mind. Sam Everett. Everett Wings. Home of six-passenger corporate jets chartered by nearly every big company in West Brook. One of the wealthiest men in the city.

Nevertheless, that did not give him the right to bark orders at her over the phone.

"I'm sorry, Mr Everett, but Marlena has gone to bed. She has an early photo session tomorrow."

"She won't have a job if she doesn't get over here! We're up against a deadline for this magazine lay-out, thanks to her, and those pictures have to go out in twelve hours!"

Slowly Codie put the receiver down

and strode to the bedroom where she tapped lightly on the door.

"Marlena, are you awake?"

"No! Go away."

"Marlena! You are wanted on the phone. A Mr Sam Everett."

"Oh, him. Tell him . . . "

"I can't, Marlena. He insists on talking to you."

Marlena opened the door and walked to the phone, "Hello, Mr Everett. I know . . . but I was so bushed . . . I see . . . Well, yes, I suppose . . . All right. Forty-five minutes."

She hung up and started for the bedroom. "I have to go to the studio or old sour-puss Everett says he'll pull his account from the agency."

"But, Marlena, you can't go all the way across town tonight. It's late. It wouldn't be safe."

"I know," Marlena's voice was muffled as she slipped a dress over her head, "but Everett's money is what is keeping Sloan Agency afloat right now. If he pulls his account, I'm

6

back to pounding the pavement for a modelling job."

Codie rubbed her slender fingers over her eyes. She was tired and she faced a long, difficult day at the university tomorrow where she was receptionist for the president, Nathan Bannister. But all that aside, she couldn't let Marlena ride a bus through the dark streets alone at such a late hour.

"I'll go with you," she said finally, her husky voice ending in a deep sigh of resignation.

"Oh, would you, Codie? That will be fun! We can talk, and you can watch me work. You'll love it."

During the bumpy bus ride to the Bev Sloan studios, Marlena managed to pull make-up from an over-sized canvas bag and deftly apply it to her soft complexion. By the time they stepped off the bus at Drake and Third, she was as beautiful as any model on the cover of *Vogue* magazine. Next to her, Codie felt frumpy in her flat-heeled shoes and faded jeans. Her smooth, oval face bore no trace of make-up. She jammed her hands deep into her jacket pockets and followed Marlena through the revolving doors into the brightly lit lobby.

Pushing through the doors of Studio B, they were met by a tall, broad-shouldered figure in cowboy boots, well-worn jeans and a rough, red plaid shirt. His rugged, tanned face was sombre; deep creases marring his forehead.

"Well, it's about time, Miss Merideth. They're set up. Get to work." Abruptly he turned away from them, covering the distance to the lighted set in long-legged strides.

"What rudeness!" fumed Codie. "Who does he think he is?"

"He's not rude, Codie," argued Marlena, "he's just used to having things done his way, in his time." She rushed toward the set to take her place before the painted backdrop of a magnificent eagle, its wings spread in regal welcome. A young man with sunglasses atop his head fussed with her hair until it was just as he wanted it.

Codie found a secluded corner out of reach of the bright lights and leaned back, her hands in her pockets, one foot pressed flat against the wall. She watched Marlena smile and turn as the cameras clicked in response. All the while, Sam Everett paced the sidelines, barking instructions, complaining when a shot wasn't to his liking.

What arrogance, inwardly complained Codie. Why doesn't he just back off and let the photographer do his job? Nothing seems to please that man! As if he had read her thoughts, Sam spun around and walked quickly to where she stood.

"Miss Merideth?"

"Yes?"

"How about finding us some coffee? We're going to be here for awhile."

Codie let her foot slide to the floor as she came to an erect position, her hazel eyes snapping with indignation. She looked up at him, ready to tell him she had no intention of being his slave. Then — in an instant — his command was softened by a broad smile as he tugged at his earlobe.

"Sorry. Didn't mean to be so demanding. It's late. Forgive me?"

His unruly, blond hair fell over his forehead, touching the perspiration that glistened there. Codie breathed in the musky fragrance of his aftershave lotion and felt a quickening of her breath, almost a gasp. She wished he would not stand so close.

"No problem," she said. "Where might I find this coffee you seem to need so badly?"

He directed a thumb over his left shoulder. "Down the hall there's a lounge. Bring the whole pot." He turned back to the set, his tall sturdiness briefly casting Codie in shadow.

Codie quickly located cups, cream and sugar which she put on a tray. With tray in one hand, coffee pot in the other, she made her way back to the studio. The fact that she was toting coffee for an arrogant, demanding self-satisfied — though unsettlingly handsome — chauvinistic male rankled her.

The tangy aroma of the hot beverage drifted across the room, drawing everyone to where she stood filling cups. The last one to approach was Sam Everett.

"Thanks," he offered mechanically as he accepted a filled cup.

"You're welcome. Your Majesty." It was a snide remark, and one she regretted the minute it had passed her soft, pink lips.

Sam's eyebrows shot up in surprise.

"Aren't we testy?" he chided.

Codie rammed her clenched fists into her pockets and gritted her teeth to hold back further retort. It would not do Marlena's position any good to alienate the man who held the Sloan Agency in the palm of his hand.

2

IT was after two in the morning before Codie and Marlena were back in their apartment. Codie undressed in a lifeless stupor, too tired to be aware of what she was doing. She set her alarm and crawled into bed.

Morning came with a jarring suddenness. Codie fought against the devilish urge to sleep the day away, finally rolling from bed and padding barefoot to the bathroom. She ran her shower cooler than normal to startle herself into action.

Running twenty minutes late, Codie rushed into her office to find Mr Bannister sitting behind her desk. Like a poorly trained seal, he was struggling to balance several phone calls at once. "Stafford University," he growled into the headset. Moving quickly, Codie hung her jacket on a hook and dropped her purse into a desk drawer. She lifted the headset from Mr Bannister's fuzz-rimmed bald head.

"Stafford University," she spoke crisply, pushing buttons and levers to channel calls to the proper phones. Mr Bannister rose and steered his short, overweight body to his office, mumbling his displeasure at having been put in such an unseemly position.

With businesslike efficiency, Codie dispensed with all the pending calls and leaned back to catch her breath. Her respite was short-lived as the phone console again began flashing its tiny lights.

"Stafford University."

"Miss Merideth?" The deep voice — the feel and flow of clear water over smooth, brown rocks — held a note of expectancy as he waited for her to respond.

"Mr Everett . . . Good morning."

"Good morning. Sorry to have kept you up so late last night, but you'll be pleased to know the photos just came out of developing and they are perfect. It was worth the late hour."

"Maybe to you," she mumbled, painfully conscious of how exhausted she felt.

"Don't you want Marlena to do well?"

"Of course."

"Then, you should be happy for her that the session went so well."

Codie drew on what little charity of spirit she could muster." Oh, I am. I am."

"Good. How about dinner tonight?"

"What?" She inhaled sharply.

"I said — would you have dinner with me tonight?"

"I'm sorry. I'm afraid I'm much too tired to be a decent dinner companion. I'm going straight home for a quick supper and early bedtime."

"I promise not to keep you out so late. Pick you up around six?"

"Hold it!" Codie snapped into the phone. "Didn't you understand me? I said I'm not interested."

"You say that now, but you'll change your mind. I promise you a quiet evening. Marlena would want you to enjoy a night out."

Like the unnerving grind of a dentist's drill, the true nature of what he was saying bore into her mind. Yes, you will go out with me, Miss Merideth, he was saying, because your sister's job depends on my good will. How dare he blackmail her like that! But she could not — no matter what the provocation — do anything to jeopardize Marlena's career.

"All right," she sighed.

"Six." Sam Everett hung up.

The rest of the day was wretched, one task not being completed before three more surfaced. By six o'clock Codie was totally spent, wanting nothing more than to go home. She fervently wished she had not succumbed to Mr Everett's tainted dinner invitation. As she draped a cover over the typewriter and switched the phone system to an answering service, the man in question opened the door, his broad shoulders moving beneath a deep brown tweed jacket. He wore sharply creased jeans and polished boots. With a confident grip, he held a white Stetson.

"Ready?" he asked, a lazy grin turning up the corners of his mouth.

"Almost." She was deliberately avoiding his gaze, not wanting to chance being swayed by those dark, sea-deep blue eyes.

"Did you wear a coat?" he asked.

She pointed toward the coat rack. He lifted her jacket from its hook and held it open for her. She stepped back toward him, her arms slipping into the sleeves. He gripped the lapels and brought them around her, his arms lingering on her shoulders. She could feel the movement of his body as he eased her against him for a brief second. He dropped his arms. Her breath caught somewhere in the back of her throat.

"Where to?" he questioned as he

held open the door for her.

"This date is your idea," she said coolly, "I should think you would have already decided."

"Then I say Harrison's for barbecued ribs and tall, tall beers."

Codie stopped abruptly, causing him nearly to step on her heels. She spun around and stared up at him in disbelief.

He frowned. "I'm sorry," he said. "Don't you like Harrison's?"

"Well, yes, I do, but . . . I'm just surprised that you do."

"Why?"

"It's not . . . well, not very . . . "

"Fancy?"

"Right. I would expect you to be more the Brossmeier's type."

His hearty laughter filled the air as he threw back his head in amusement. "Me? I'm afraid Brossmeier's is much too snobbish for me."

Again he took her arm, guiding her toward a sleek, silver-grey Jaguar parked in a no-parking zone at the kerb. He held the door open; Codie slid into the plush red interior and leaned her head back against the seat. Weariness slowly eased from her. Sam climbed in, extending his long legs beneath the wheel, and turned the key in the ignition. He twisted around to face her.

"Well? Harrison's?"

"Harrison's."

Apparently she had misjudged Sam Everett. That he would prefer the casual comfort of a barbecue place to the sophisticated trappings of Brossmeier's said more about him than his sleek Jaguar or all his charter jets. She settled into the cosy luxury of the seat and enjoyed the passing lights of the city as they sped toward Harrison's. Once inside the garish, poorly lit restaurant, they elbowed their way through the crowd to a corner booth. Sam waited until she was seated then slid in beside her. A waitress made her way toward them. Without asking permission, Sam ordered for both of them.

18

Their food was not long in coming: Texas toast, a platter piled high with ribs, and cold, sweating glasses of beer. When the waitress had gone, Sam turned toward Codie, slipping his arm across the back of the booth. Stifled by his aggressiveness, Codie clasped her hands in her lap.

"Forgive my forwardness," he said, "but in here, if you don't sit close, you can't hear a word." Codie relaxed, ashamed of her silent accusations.

"Don't try to be too neat," Sam said. "With the ribs. If you try to be neat and proper, you'll starve. Just grab one and dig in."

Gingerly Codie picked up a plump, juicy rib and lifted it to her mouth. She bit down on the smoky meat and felt liquid trickle down her chin. Sam yanked a paper napkin from the metal canister and dabbed away the spicy sauce.

"You'll get the hang of it," he chuckled. "Just remember, don't try . . ."

"I know. Don't try to be neat."

Many ribs, and dozens of paper napkins later, Codie relaxed into the corner of the booth and silently whistled.

"I'll never eat again!"

"Oh, you will," laughed Sam. "This won't last forever."

"How can you say that?" she countered, rubbing sticky fingers on yet another napkin. Sam took the napkin from her and tossed it on the table.

"Don't rub all the flavour away." He held her fingers between his strong, firm hands. Lifting them to his lips, he tenderly kissed the tip of each one, the magical blue of his eyes drawing her into their depths. As his lips touched her flesh, Codie felt the tingling flutter along her arms; felt the heat touch her cheeks. She lowered her eyes, trying to escape the intimacy of his gaze. Then suddenly she jerked her hands away. She knew she was there for only one reason, to protect Marlena's job. It would be foolish to pretend otherwise. Sensing her rejection, Sam turned sharply from her and signalled for the waitress.

"Check, please," he told the young girl. Then, tossing several coins under the edge of his plate, he stood and held out his hand. "Shall we go?" the misty softness had left his eyes.

In the car, Codie rode in silence, not certain of Sam's mood. In Harrison's, when he had held her hands, touching his lips to her fingertips, she had seen in his eyes an unveiled, undemanding gentleness. Now he seemed to have closed a door between them.

Inwardly, Codie battled against the emptiness his distance caused her. It had been folly to imagine Sam Everett could be anything but a self-serving, spoiled brat of wealth. She folded her arms and leaned back, refusing to cater to his moodiness. Sam spoke only once, to ask for her address.

When he brought the Jaguar to a stop in front of the apartment building, he sat staring straight ahead, his hands gripping the leather steering wheel. Codie swallowed hard to relieve the tension that had built inside her. The urge to jump from the car without a word (a fitting response to his manner) fought against her deep-seated sense of propriety.

"Thank you," she said. "I enjoyed dinner." She could not lie and tell him the entire evening had been a pleasure. She resented his having ruined it for her. Sam turned his head toward her, looking at her through half-closed eyes.

"Am I such a bad guy, Codie?"

She unfolded her arms and moved around to lean her back against the door. "I don't know what you mean."

"We were having a good time back there, weren't we?" he asked in a gruff voice.

"Yes . . . yes. We were."

"Then, why the sudden turn-off?" He raised his hands from the wheel and ran them through his hair.

Codie sighed heavily. "We both know

why you asked me to dinner — and why I accepted. It would be silly to read any more into it than that."

"Whoa! Whoa!" Sam held up a hand as if to ward off her words. "What are you talking about?"

She looked away from him to allow her heart to quiet its fluttering; allow her mind to return to rational thinking.

"Codie," he insisted, "what are you talking about?"

She clenched her fists to bolster her confidence. "You made it very clear on the phone. I was blackmailed."

A broad grin quickly worked its way across his face. He put a hand on her shoulder. "Blackmailed? How in the world did I do that?"

She was angry at Sam for pretending he was not aware of his own deceitfulness, and at herself for falling into his trap. "Oh, Sam, come on! I'm twenty-six years old. I've heard every line in the book. But, I must say, your approach does have one thing going for it. It can't fail."

23

Sam's cheeks puffed out and he blew air through pursed lips.

"I sure wish I knew what you're driving at."

"Let it drop, Sam." She opened the door. "Thank you for the rites." As she climbed out and started up the steps she fumbled in her purse for her keys. Footsteps sounded behind her. Sam grabbed her arm and spun her around.

"All right, Miss Merideth, let's have it. What's got you all fired up?"

She felt the pressure of his fingers through her jacket and tried to deny the sensation it sent along her arm. "All right, you knew I would not do anything that would endanger Marlena's very shaky career. I understood, Mr Everett, and so I went. Blackmail."

His grip first tightened, then went slack. Codie saw his brows draw together over dark, brooding eyes. Dropping his hand to his side, he turned on the hard, polished heels of his boots and descended the steps two

24

at a time. Codie watched as he jerked open the car door and climbed in. She turned and forced the key into the lock. When she looked back, the sleek, silver-grey Jaguar was rounding the corner, tyres squealing on the pavement.

3

THE next morning dawned cold and dreary, mist hanging in the air like soggy cellophane. Codie pulled the covers over her head and silently thanked God it was Saturday. Groggy peacefulness lulled her back to sleep. Two hours later she awoke to the sound of the shower.

Marlena came out of the bathroom wrapped in a new plush terry towel the size of a beach blanket. Codie pushed herself upright against the headboard and drew up her knees. "New towel?" she yawned.

"Yeah. Isn't it plushy?"

"Um. How much did it cost?"

"Not much." Marlena tossed the towel onto the bed.

Codie frowned. "How much, Lenie?"

"It was on sale."

"Marlena!" Codie jumped from

beneath the covers and grabbed her robe. "That towel was an unnecessary expense. We cannot afford it. You do not need it."

"Oh, but I do, Codie. It's important to my image."

"Your image? Your image? Who's going to see you?" Codie tugged angrily at the sash of her robe.

"It makes me feel good. And, when I feel good, I do good."

Codie scowled.

"So . . . that's bad grammar. But it's important to me. I have to feel right."

Codie shot her sister a burning glance and stormed out of the room. How dare Marlena squander their meagre funds. It meant that now, instead of the roast and potatoes she had planned for Marlena's birthday dinner next week, it would be meatloaf stretched with breadcrumbs — again. It meant day-old sugar cookies instead of French vanilla ice cream for dessert. How dare she!

At breakfast, Marlena sipped weak tea and nibbled on dry toast.

"You really should eat more than that, Marlena," warned Codie. "You can't function without breakfast."

"It's all I need. If I gain even one pound, they'll start looking for someone else."

Codie sighed, "Suit yourself." She finished her scrambled eggs and pushed back her plate. "Want to attend church with me tomorrow?" It was a question she asked every Saturday; a question her sister always answered the same.

"Naw. You go," she chortled, "and pray for me."

"I always do, Lenie."

Marlena lowered her eyes in a brief moment of pretended repentance then looked up with a grin. "Thanks, Codie. I know God listens to you better than He does to me."

"He listens to everyone."

"Well," Marlena said as she pushed back from the table, "right now I don't have a whole lot to say to Him. Want to go for a walk with me?"

"No, thanks. I want to clean the apartment."

"Okay. I'll be back in about an hour." Marlena slipped into a jacket as she breezed out the door. Codie cleared the table and put the dishes to soak. Then, after dressing hurriedly in patched jeans and her favourite tattered flannel shirt, on hands and knees, she began scrubbing the kitchen floor. Just as she was giving it a final rinse with clear water, a sharp rap sounded at the door. Codie stood, wiping her hands on her jeans.

"Who is it?" she called out.

"Sam Everett."

No! She put water-wrinkled fingers to her mussed hair and glanced down at her rumpled jeans and tattered shirt. Where could she hide? She walked toward the door.

"Codie?" came his voice again. "Are you there?"

"Yes." Fingers shaking, she turned the lock. "Come in," she mumbled, stepping back to allow him room to enter.

"Did I come at a bad time?" he asked as his eyes took in her sloppy appearance.

"No. I'm just . . . " She pointed toward the kitchen, " . . . just scrubbing . . . " Her hands brushed again at her hair. "Please, sit down. Coffee?"

Sam tossed his Stetson toward a chair. "No, thanks. I just came by to see if you wanted to ride to Chicago with me."

"Chicago?" Codie forgot her unsightliness. "Chicago? That's a day's drive from here. Why would you . . . ?"

He put a finger to her lips. "Shh. Now, listen. How would the owner of Everett Wings travel . . . by *car*?"

"Oh." She sat down on the sofa, unconsciously making room for him to sit beside her. "Of course. You would fly. Why are you going to Chicago?"

"To pick up a new plane. Interested?"

"Oh, I don't know. Sam. It's cleaning

day . . . It doesn't seem like a good idea."

Turning sideways toward her, he brought one scuffed boot onto his opposite knee, his hand resting on its soft, worn leather. "Are you still cross with me for the boorish way I behaved last night?"

Codie shook her head.

"I promise, we'll be back in plenty of time. The cleaning can wait until then, can't it?"

Codie tugged at the tail of her shirt as if to hide her patched jeans. "I'd need some time to get ready."

He jumped up. "Wish granted. I'll be back in an hour."

Grabbing his hat, he strode quickly through the door. Amazed at her acceptance of his invitation, and that she could so easily forgive him last night, Codie stepped into the shower. What was she thinking? She could not fly to Chicago with Sam Everett. It was foolhardy even to consider it. Vowing to call and cancel, she turned off the water. She remembered Marlena's plushy new towel and something inside her rebelled. She would go!

At the end of an hour, Codie sat in the living room waiting for Sam. She had written a note to Marlena and taped it to the refrigerator.

"Codie?" Sam called from the other side of the door.

She opened the door. "Hello," she whispered huskily, too excited to say more.

"Hi. You look great. Quite a transformation. Let's go."

Downstairs, sitting like an earthbound bird, was the Jaguar. Standing next to it was Marlena, gaping wide-eyed at its magnificence. She didn't turn around as they approached.

"Like it?" asked Sam.

"Mr Everett! Is this yours?" She seemed unaware of Codie's presence.

"Sure is."

"It's so, so spiffy. I'd love to ride in it." She looked up at him from under long, fluttering dark lashes.

"Sure. Some time," agreed Sam. "Right now this young lady and I are in a rush to get to the airport."

Marlena looked around. "Codie? Where are you going?"

"Chicago."

Sam helped Codie into the car, then spun the car into the flow of traffic. Looking back, Codie saw Marlena still standing at the kerb, her mouth open in astonishment.

Codie gasped in awe at the sight of the glistening row of jets, EVERETT WINGS emblazoned in bright blue across their slender bodies.

"Why should you need another plane?" she asked. "It looks as if you have more than enough."

"I never have enough, Codie. As long as there is one corporation in West Brook I can't service because of a lack of jets, I don't have enough. See that one, third from the left?"

"The one with the bright yellow tail?"

"Um — hum. That's all mine. No

one flies that one but me."

"It's beautiful. Is that the one we'll be taking?"

"No, no. We're taking a trade-in. No way would I trade in Golden Eagle."

Codie glanced at him, surprised at the little-boy glow in his cheeks and the bright shine of his blue, blue eyes. Apparently, for Sam Everett, there was no pleasure to match that of flying. A mechanic in greasy coveralls walked up to the car.

"Morning, Mr Everett," he said, "it's all spruced up for you."

"Thanks, Dirk. This is Miss Merideth."

Codie nodded and smiled. Dirk rushed around to open the door for her. "Glad to meet you, Miss Merideth."

The three of them walked out to the plane, Dirk giving Sam a rapid-fire accounting of the ground check the jet had received. Sam nodded in approval.

"Sounds good, Dirk, ole buddy. Hate to see this bird go. It's been a good one."

"Sure has, Mr Everett. I'll get Randall."

"Why do you have to get rid of it?" Codie asked, sensing Sam's reluctance in letting it go.

"It's time. My business depends on getting clients where they want to go — rapidly and all in one piece."

Codie felt a cold knot twist itself low in her stomach. "You mean this plane may not get us to Chicago?"

Sam put a firm, reassuring arm around her shoulders. "It'll get us there, Miss Merideth. I guarantee it." They walked toward the open hatch, Sam's arm still around her, and climbed the portable stairway. Inside, Sam led her back to the body of the plane where thickly cushioned swivel chairs were anchored to the floor, each one flanked by a tiny round table.

"How fabulous!" whispered Codie. "I could travel around the world in a plane like this."

"Sounds good," Sam teased. "I'll

tell the pilot not to touch down in Chicago."

Codie sat down in one of the chairs and leaned against its back. She looked up at Sam in surprise. "Pilot? Aren't you flying this thing?"

"Not this time. Thought I'd ride back here with the passenger." He reached across her lap to fasten her seat belt. His sun-kissed blond hair was only a breath away from her. She inhaled his sweet outdoors smell and felt weakness overtake her limbs.

A short, stocky man wearing a bright yellow Everett Wings jacket, entered the plane and, after allowing another man to enter, strong-armed the hatch closed. "Hi there, Sam," he said. "Ready?"

"We're ready. Randall, this is Miss Merideth. Codie, meet our pilot, Pete Randall and our co-pilot Stiff Burton."

The plane taxied to the end of the runway, the roar of the jets increasing with each passing second. When the roar reached an anxious whine, the plane inched forward then it lifted,

36

pointing its nose toward Chicago.

"You can unfasten your belt now," Sam said. "We're up. What would you like to drink?"

Codie spun her chair around to face him. "What are my choices?"

"Anything you like."

"I'll have ginger-ale, please."

"Nothing in it?"

"No, thanks. Things are heady enough as it is."

Ice crackled in the glasses as he filled them with bubbling ginger-ale. When he sat down, he swung his chair around, his knees brushing hers. She shifted slightly to give him more room.

"I don't bite, Codie," he said. "Why are you always pulling away from me?"

"I'm not." She took a long, slow sip from her drink.

"Oh, no? Watch this." He leaned forward and put a hand on her knee. Instinctively, Codie swung out of his reach. "See?" he accused.

Codie stood and walked to the

window. The sun seemed within arm's reach, spilling its brilliant rays over the clouds in waves of gold. Codie felt her body sway with the gentle pitch of the plane.

"I'll never understand," she whispered huskily, "how something like this stays in the air. It goes against everything I understand about gravity."

"It's the currents of air over the wings," Sam said. "The wings spread wide over the air; the jets push them forward and the air supports them. Like an invisible god with very big hands."

Codie noticed the change in his tone and turned.

He was looking at her, his eyes misty soft, holding her in their amorous grip. He put his hands on her waist and pulled her close. She felt the strength of his muscles as he wrapped his arms about her and nestled his cheek in her hair. His warm breath seeped into her, torturing her with its passion.

"Codie . . . Codie . . . " Tenderly

he touched her cheek, letting his hand slide to the warm flesh of her neck. His fingers locked in the soft curls at her nape as he brought his lips to meet hers. The feel of his mouth stole her strength, leaving her breathless, unable to resist. When finally he released her, she clasped her hands behind her and leaned against the cabin wall.

"Sam . . . "

"I know. I shouldn't have done that."

"I'm not in your league, Sam. I live in a world of simple integrity and hard work. I don't know what it's like to have everything around me programmed to meet my every need, to adjust to my every whim."

He moved to the opposite side of the cabin where he sat down, his legs extended lazily, boots crossed at the ankles. "What are you saying, Codie? I don't have integrity?"

"Not the same kind. You see something you want, and you go about getting it. With me, I have to consider how it affects everyone around me. It's the only way I know."

"You think I don't consider anyone else, is that it?" His eyes held her gaze, locked in silent battle as he challenged her.

"I'm just saying we approach things differently. I have to decide between pot roast and a beach towel. You can buy the beach."

His eyes grew wide as he laughed. "Beach towel? What in the world are you talking about?"

"Nothing. You wouldn't understand."

"Try me."

"Marlena bought a very expensive towel the size of the state of Nebraska, which means there won't be money for the dinner I had planned for her birthday." Codie paced absentmindedly from one end of the cabin to the other. "Choices. I have to make them every day. There's never quite enough."

She was not prepared for the steel-hard tension that clamped itself in his jaw. His eyes turned sharp, cold blue-green. Codie quickly dismissed what she had said. "But! Not to worry. Marlena and I do fine. and, some day, when she makes it big with the Sloan Agency, we'll be on easy street. Is there any more of that ginger-ale?"

She hadn't finished the first one but she needed something to erase the pity she imagined was behind his steady gaze.

"Why are you doing it?" he asked as he filled two fresh glasses. "Staying with Marlena."

"She needs me. She has to be free to go on assignments, to take advantage of every opportunity."

"What about you? I understand you gave up something you wanted pretty badly to come to the city. Doesn't that count for anything?"

"I have wanted only one thing, to help — really help," she countered as she accepted the cold glass. "If that means helping Marlena," she shrugged, "then that's what I'll do."

"What if, after you support her for a year, two years, she still doesn't make the big time? What do you do then, Miss Codie Merideth?"

"Go back to where I was."

"Rock Creek?"

"Not necessarily. I'll start again."

The tension came back to his jaw and, without a word, he turned and strode to the cockpit where he disappeared through the narrow door. Codie sat down and waited.

Some time later, a chime sounded and a flashing light signalled for her to fasten her seat belt. The plane banked to the left and began its descent. Codie's ears popped then throbbed. She closed her eyes against the pain.

"Open your mouth," he said. She had not heard him come in. "Yawn as wide as you can." She opened only one eye, not wanting to antagonize the pain. "Go on," he ordered. "Yawn."

Feeling silly, she opened her mouth wide and forced a yawn. Her ears popped again and the pain began to ease. She smiled a thank you.

"Again," he insisted. "Do it again."

She obeyed. Her ears opened even further, relieving the pain completely. "Thanks. Aren't you supposed to be buckled in?"

"We're almost down. I'll be all right."

Just at that moment the plane gave a quick, unsteady jerk, throwing Sam in a sprawling heap on the carpeted floor. Codie snickered. Then, when he glared up at her with a don't-you-dare-laugh scowl, she broke into uncontrolled laughter.

He struggled to a sitting position and worked his way into one of the chairs. "Stop laughing," he threatened, "or I'll pour that drink down your pretty little neck."

She clamped a hand over her mouth, her eyes alive with unexpressed giggling.

"You tell Randall about this and you're in big trouble."

"Oh, I won't!" she promised, holding

up her hand in silent oath. "I won't say a word."

Randall emerged from the cockpit and opened the hatch. Someone on the ground rolled portable stairs to the opening.

"When will you want to be starting back, Sam?" Randall asked as they descended the stairs.

"New plane should be ready by seven o'clock. We'll meet you back here at Midway around six-thirty."

Sam took Codie's arm and guided her toward the terminal. He signalled a skycap and asked him to summon a cab for them.

The cab driver stood holding the door for them, no doubt expecting the same generous tip given the skycap. He wasn't disappointed.

"See what I mean?" Codie asked as they settled into the seat. "You just gave those two men more money than I have ever spent on . . . "

"Come on, Codie, don't start that again, okay?"

She glanced at him to see if his mood matched his tone: troubled, a little distressed. He smiled. "Let's not talk money. Let's talk about what we're going to do for the next five or six hours."

"I'm in your hands, Mr Everett. I've never been to Chicago in my life."

"You're kidding! Well, that certainly opens up a lot of possibilities. How about if we start with lunch? I'm famished."

Codie realized for the first time that she, too, was more than a little hungry. Sam leaned forward and spoke to the cab driver.

"How does seafood sound?" Sam asked, putting an arm across the back of the seat.

"Fine by me."

Nearly an hour later the cab came to a halt in front of an elaborate, thirty-storey building that bore all the markings of an architectural masterpiece from a time past. Codie marvelled at its ornate, dark-stone façade and flamboyant marquee.

As Sam paid the driver, she stood gawking childlike at its magnificence. An unobtrusive brass plaque identified the building as one of Chicago's finest hotels.

Once inside the munificently furnished lobby, they crossed the carpeted floor to doors that opened into a softly lit dining room. A burning candle sat on each white covered table, belying the midday sun that shone just outside. Codie felt she had, at that moment, an acute understanding of how Alice must have felt when she entered Wonderland.

4

LUNCH stretched on into the afternoon as they tried one seafood delicacy after another. At last, Codie begged a reprieve.

"Please, Sam, no more!"

"But you haven't tried the . . . "

"No! No!" She reached over to press her fingers to his lips. "Say no more. I can't bear another bite."

"Well, if you're sure," Sam frowned playfully. "In that case . . . " He signalled for the waiter. "We'll be on our way." He slipped the waiter several crisp bills and stood up.

The afternoon was fleet of foot, passing much too quickly as they talked, sharing dreams that lay within their hearts. For the first time, Codie spoke aloud of her vision of a loving home for children. Sam seemed to absorb the dream into himself, touching

Codie's cheek softly as he did so.

They visited a museum, two art galleries, a park where children rode tiny ponies, and a cafe that specialized in sinfully rich desserts. Once again in a cab, Codie rested back against the seat, her eyes closed in contentment.

"Have fun?" asked Sam.

"Oh, yes, this is quite a city."

"There are a lot of great cities, Codie. Maybe we'll see them all eventually."

The cab stopped in front of the hotel where, what seemed a lifetime ago, they had enjoyed lunch. Codie raised her eyebrows.

"This won't take a minute. I need to make a phone call. Want to wait inside?"

Sam strode to the front desk and lifted the receiver of one of the telephones. As he talked, he half-turned toward her and winked. She smiled, sensing the touch the gesture implied.

Sam turned his full attention to the phone, his voice rising in agitation as he argued with the party on the other end. He dropped the receiver in place and came toward her, shrugging his shoulders.

"I'm sorry, Codie. I'm afraid my new plane won't be ready until morning."

"What?" Codie jumped up. "What are we going to do?"

"Stay over. It's our only choice."

"Oh, now wait just a minute . . . You promised you would get me back tonight. I have no intention of staying in Chicago."

"Come on, Codie. Be reasonable. I never take up a plane unless I know it's in top-notch condition. I'm not leaving the ground unless that plane is ready."

"But, it's brand new! How could anything be wrong with it?"

"There's a loose connection in the fuel line."

"How long can that take?"

"Not long, but . . . "

"I see." Codie folded her arms in begrudging acceptance. "You're going to have to up-date your line, Everett. This one is rusty."

Sam's anger matched hers. "Is that what you think this is? I'm a pilot, not a desperate Romeo." He returned to the desk where he spoke with the clerk then signed the guest register. Codie clamped her jaw in stubborn determination. As he approached, she lowered her eyes sheepishly. He was holding up two keys.

"I'll show you to your room, Miss Merideth . . . if that's all right."

They didn't speak as the elevator zipped to the twenty-first floor. The doors swooshed open and they stepped out onto thick maroon carpeting. Sam stopped at 2109 and inserted one of the keys in the lock. Turning the knob, he pushed back the door and gave a sweeping bow.

"Your room, Miss Merideth. Will there be anything else?"

She took the key and walked past him into the lavishly furnished room. Floor-to-ceiling windows looked out over the city. Without turning, she dismissed him.

"That will be all. I won't be needing you any further."

She heard the door close behind him.

After slipping the safety chain into its slot, she stood in the middle of the room, fussing over her predicament. She was in a strange city with not so much as a toothbrush; and her sister would be alone in their apartment for the first time since they had moved to West Brook. She kicked off her shoes and fell back across the bed.

Sedated by the rich foods she had eaten and the quietness of the room, she drifted off to sleep. In her dreams, she was soaring high above the clouds on the wide, golden wings of an eagle. She could feel the breeze across her cheeks and smell the fresh clean air.

She awoke suddenly. The room was dark. Outside the windows, the city lights sparkled against the blackness. She stretched her arms above her head, trying to ease her cramped muscles. She rolled over and glanced at the clock.

"Nine o'clock! I've got to call Marlena." While Codie waited for the connection to be made, she thought of Sam.

"I won't be needing you any further," she had said to him. He must have taken her at her word.

The news didn't set well with Marlena. She had never spent a night alone in her life. "I can't be here alone, Codie!"

"Okay, Marlena. I'll see what I can do. I'll call you later."

Codie didn't have enough money to fly back to West Brook on a commercial flight and the idea of asking Sam for the money was unthinkable. She felt alone and helpless. She phoned room service for coffee. At least she could afford that.

A knock sounded at the door. Standing in the hall, his arms loaded with sacks and boxes, was Sam.

"Let me in," he groaned, "the one in the middle is slipping." He staggered in and dumped the packages on the bed.

"That should hold you," he said, flexing his arms now freed of their burden.

"What's this?" Codie wanted to know

"Oh, toothbrush, shampoo, nightgown, slippers, jeans, boots . . . shall I go on?"

"No . . . no. That's fine." She stood looking down at the clutter on the bed.

While she had been grousing about the impossible circumstances they were in, he had been considering her comfort. Her anger dissolved like a billowy cloud in the wind.

"Thank you, Sam."

"No problem. Are you sure you're a size sixteen large?"

She swung around at him, but he grabbed her wrists and held them to her sides.

"Oh, no you don't," he chuckled.

"I'm not about to wind up on the floor for the second time in one day." He released her arms and stepped away from her, pushing his Stetson back on his head. "If there's anything that isn't there, blame the salesclerk. She said that is everything you could possibly want, even if you stayed a week." From the hallway, he looked back over his shoulder as she was pushing the door closed. "Good-night, Codie."

Her reply was barely a whisper, husky and warm, "Good-night, Sam."

There was everything from toothpaste to magazines. There was even a plushy, terry bath towel with 'Nebraska' scrolled across it in mammoth red letters.

The nightgown took her breath away. It was filmy soft, the colour of rich cream. She pressed it to her cheek and marvelled at its touch.

To wear over the gown was a matching satin peignoir. Codie hugged them both to her and ran to the bathroom to fill the tub with steaming hot water, luxuriously lacing it with Sam's choice of bubble bath, Gardenia Silk.

All thoughts of going home to West Brook, and to Marlena, were lost in the sweet-smelling vapours that rose to engulf her as she slid beneath the water, her first truly hot bath in months.

Three sharp raps at the door marred her reverie.

"Room service," came a muffled voice.

At the door, she looked through the tiny peephole then unfastened the chain, standing hidden behind the door as she opened it. A tray came into view.

The tray was lowered to the floor. "Sign here, please."

Codie took the ticket in her wet hands and hurriedly signed her name, adding what she hoped was an appropriate tip. Sam's extravagance made it difficult to be rational. She moved the laden tray to a table by the window, torn between allowing the coffee or her bath to get cold. She gave in to the sweet aroma emanating from the silver carafe and quickly donned the billowy gown and peignoir. It was while she sat sipping coffee from a china cup that she remembered Marlena and the promise she had made to her.

It was too late now to return to West Brook. How could her sister ever forgive her? She had allowed the lavishness showered on her by Sam Everett to cloud her sense of duty.

She had failed Marlena and therefore she was failing herself, for she was not doing what was expected of her.

Early the next morning Codie was still bearing the guilt of her self-indulgence. She picked up the phone and dialled.

"Front desk," came the response.

"This is Miss Merideth in 2109. Could you tell me where the nearest chapel is?"

There was a rustling of pages on the other end of the line as the desk clerk searched for the information.

"Just three blocks west," he said. "It's nondenominational, small. Shall I look further?"

"No, no," answered Codie. "That will be just fine."

It was a long talk with God in the small chapel. Codie struggled with the guilt of her momentary lapse in liability, her disregard for her sister. Sorrow poured over her as she realized how close she had come to allowing pleasure to overshadow her sense of duty. She vowed to make amends.

She strode back to the hotel feeling less burdened. And there, his feet widespread, hands on his hips, stood Sam. A deep, sombre scowl drew furrows in his brow.

"Where have you been?" he demanded in a whispered growl.

Codie bristled under his verbal assault. "I beg your pardon!"

"You weren't in your room. I thought . . . " He ran fingers through his hair. "Well, never mind what I thought. What are you doing out at this hour, alone?"

Shoulders erect, Codie walked past him toward the elevator.

"I'm capable of taking care of myself."

"Maybe so, but you don't know Chicago." He was following her, his voice still gruff. "You should have let me know where you were going, Codie. I could have gone with you."

"It never occurred to me that you would be interested in visiting a chapel." She began to feel a little ashamed that she had not at least given him the opportunity to join her. Her voice softened, "I'm sorry."

He punched the button for the twenty-first floor. "You're a tough lady, Codie Merideth. What makes you so independent?"

"The need to survive."

"You'll survive. Can't you let go just a little? Let someone else share the load?"

"This is between me and God, Sam. We'll handle it."

When the car stopped at their floor, Sam held his thumb on the 'Closed' button, preventing the doors from opening.

"Had breakfast?" he asked.

"Not yet."

His thumb moved to the button marked 'Lobby' and the elevator started down again. Codie sighed. She would give him this one, but he was going to have to learn that she could not be controlled; could not be manipulated by his power.

5

SAM once again called the airport. At last, the plane was ready. He and Codie went quickly to their rooms to pack. She changed into the jeans, sweater and boots and put her rumpled outfit in a sack. She stepped out just as Sam was emerging from his room.

"There'll be a room service charge and a phone call on my bill," she told him.

"Okay." His manner was stilted.

The cab ride to the airport was made in silence. Sam spoke only to the driver and that was in a clipped, monosyllabic tone. Codie chalked it up to his spoiled nature. On the plane, she slept most of the trip back to West Brook. Sam drove her to the apartment and waited as she climbed out of the car with her packages. She felt obligated to mention them.

"Thank you for the supplies."

"You're welcome."

He shifted gears and pulled away from the kerb. Codie turned and walked up the steps, remembering with disappointment that she had left the Nebraska towel in the hotel bathroom.

Marlena was asleep on the living room sofa. Codie closed the door carefully, not wanting to wake her. She hadn't counted on the packages slipping from her grasp and falling to the floor.

Marlena jerked to an upright position. "Codie? Where've you been?"

Codie was beginning to chafe under so much interrogation. "We had some plane trouble. I told you that on the phone."

"You also told me you would come home last night," Marlena pouted. "It was awful here by myself. What's in the bags?"

Codie picked up the packages and tossed them on a chair.

"Supplies," she said, kicking off her boots.

"You sure are grumpy."

"Sorry. It's been a long day. I got up early to go to church."

"You're kidding. In Chicago? Who was there to see you?"

Marlena disentangled herself and padded into the bedroom. Codie went into the kitchen to heat water for tea. Her head was pounding and she hoped it would ease the ache.

Only a trickle of water flowed into the kettle. Marlena must have turned on the shower. Codie lowered her head between her arms. Tears burned hot in her eyes. How hard it was going to be to forget the past twenty-four hours.

But she would. She *had* to forget.

★ ★ ★

Ensuing days seemed to weave in and out of each other like a patchwork quilt. Codie rose early, went to the office, came home and prepared dinner.

62

By bedtime she was exhausted and uncommunicative. As the day of Marlena's birthday neared, Codie pushed herself harder and harder to overcome her mood. Marlena was like a little girl, pretending she didn't know it was her birthday, yet dropping hints. On the actual day, Codie left work early to have time to prepare supper before Marlena got home. She was just taking the meatloaf from the oven when her sister came in.

"Ooh, Codie, it smells delicious. What is it?"

"Meatloaf, macaroni and cheese."

"Oh."

As they ate, Marlena told Codie about her day's assignment, a word-by-word accounting of what it was like to stand before cameras while wearing a full-length sable coat and thousands of dollars worth of diamonds.

"It was incredible, Codie," beamed Marlena. "I felt like a princess."

Codie smiled. "It must have been nice."

"Oh, it was. I could really learn to like being rich, Codie. It feels so good."

"I'm sure it does." Visions of a posh Chicago hotel with huge brass doors and thick, thick carpeting flashed across Codie's mind, digging deep furrows of longing into her consciousness.

"Gee, Codie, you were a million miles away."

"Sorry. Ready for dessert?"

In a rash moment, Codie had bought the French vanilla ice cream after all.

"Ooh," moaned Marlena with pleasure.

Codie dipped generous mounds into dessert dishes and set them on the table. "Happy birthday, Lenie," she smiled, dipping her spoon into the rich, creamy dessert. But she couldn't swallow it. It wouldn't slide past the lump in her throat.

★ ★ ★

A whole week had gone by since Codie's trip to Chicago. Sam had not called her once. Not a word. It was as if, for him, she no longer existed. Codie tried hard to forget Sam Everett.

She had been the one who had said they were in different leagues. She was the one who had turned a cold shoulder to his concern for her whereabouts.

When nearly two weeks had passed and still he hadn't called, she accepted what had to be and tried to get on with her life. Assignments for Marlena were coming more and more frequently and, as a result, their bank account began to take on the look of serious savings. For brief moments at a time, Codie allowed herself to believe that she could start planning to return to Rock Creek.

One evening Codie was just settling into a corner of the sofa to read when the phone rang.

"Codie?"

Her heart leaped in a frenzy of excitement. His voice washed over her like the music of a clear, flowing stream. "Hello, Sam."

"Thought we'd go out for a bite to

eat. How about it?"

The beating of her heart settled into an angry thumping against her ribs. What nerve! To call after so long and expect her to just jump at his invitation!

"Real clever, Mr Everett," she snapped.

"Hey, what's up? I just asked if you wanted to go out to eat."

"No thank you. I've already eaten."

"So . . . how about coffee and some sinfully rich dessert?"

"No."

"Okay, Codie," his voice lost its teasing manner. "What's wrong?"

"Wrong? You drive off in a huff and don't call for two weeks, then you expect . . . "

"Hold it. Hold it. That's not how it was."

"Oh, no? Then how was it, Sam?"

"Let me come by. We'll talk about it."

"Sorry. I'm busy."

"You certainly have a lot to learn

about charity, Miss Merideth." And with that, he hung up.

Codie held the phone pressed to her cheek. Tears spilled from her eyes and she let herself cry, pouring out all her frustration.

On Sunday, Marlena rose early to have breakfast with Codie.

"You wouldn't believe it, Codie, the way those people expect you to just 'hop to' whenever they call."

"Some people are like that. They have to have everything their way, in their time," mumbled Codie.

"I have to admit. I love it!" Marlena giggled, "This is what I want to do, Codie. And I know I'm going to make it big. Sam thinks so."

"Sam?" Codie took in a deep breath. "You've seen Sam?"

"Yeah. We're doing another magazine lay-out. He sure had a wild trip, did he tell you?"

"Uh, no . . . " Codie's mind kept stumbling over visions of Sam. "What trip?"

"To Alaska. Well, it was pretty scary. He flew a couple of oil men up to Alaska to look at some wells or something. When they got ready to come back, Sam found something wrong with the plane and told them he wouldn't start back until it was fixed."

A cold, tight knot twisted in Codie's stomach. "Sam wouldn't fly a plane that wasn't ready," she offered.

"No, but these men were furious. They had to get back for some important conference, and made Sam take off."

"I can't believe he would do that."

"He said he wouldn't have ordinarily, but he was as anxious to get back as they were. They didn't get far when the plane stalled out and they made an emergency landing."

Codie waited for Marlena to continue, near hysteria throbbing in her head. She knew Sam was all right but she couldn't bear what he must have gone through.

"I can't believe Sam hasn't told you about this," Marlena said. "They stayed in the plane for two days waiting for someone to find them. It must have been awful."

Codie rested her elbows on the table and buried her head in her hands. Far back in her mind was a curious nagging. Why hadn't he told her he was going out of town.

Marlena worked long, late hours, coming in for five or six hours' sleep then going out again. On Thursday it was after midnight when she finally got home.

"Codie! Codie! Wake up."

Codie moaned, "Don't do this, Marlena."

"Wake up! I have something to tell you!"

Codie turned on her back and squeezed her eyes shut against the bright light. "This had better be good, Lenie."

"It is. Look at me!"

Codie opened one eye.

Marlena held out a bright red and white airline ticket. "Codie, I'm going to Europe!"

"What?" Codie sat up and rubbed her eyes.

"I'm going to Europe. Can you believe it?"

"When?"

"In the morning."

"For how long?"

"Three months. Remember all those furs and diamonds I told you about?"

Codie nodded.

"The company wants to do a spread in Paris and one in London. Three models were chosen to go and," she lifted her chin and struck an elaborate pose, "I'm one."

"Oh, Marlena, that is fantastic." Codie patted the side of the bed. "Sit down. Tell me everything."

She went with Marlena to the airport then directly to the university. Codie sat down at the typewriter and wrote out her letter of resignation, giving two weeks' notice.

6

TWO weeks later, Codie withdrew her half of the savings from the bank and closed up the apartment, leaving a letter to Marlena on the table. By noon she was on her way to the Ozarks.

Codie knew she could not give up the apartment until Marlena returned but, with what they had saved, she felt she could manage until she could find a job.

The bus ride was long. When they arrived, the sun had gone down behind the mountains, spreading dusk in a soft blanket over the town. Codie was the only one to disembark. She stood on the sidewalk and looked about for a cab. When none appeared, she went inside the small cabin that served as a terminal. A sleepy-eyed old man in a tan uniform sat behind a small grilled window. Codie tapped her knuckles lightly on the countertop.

"Huh?" The old man came forward in his chair.

"Could you call me a cab, please?" she asked.

"No need. I can take you wherever you want to go."

"Thank you. I need to find a room."

The old man rose and came around his caged cubicle. "I can take you to the Mountain View Hotel, or to Mizz Oldham's Bed 'n' Breakfast."

"I'll take the Bed 'n' Breakfast."

"Okey-dokey," yawned the old man as he picked up her luggage, struggling under its weight.

They rode to Miss Oldham's in a battered muddy jeep. When it came to a rumbling halt in front of the Bed 'n' Breakfast, Codie opened her purse.

"How much?" she asked.

"No charge, Miss. Glad to do it."

Codie smiled and stepped out. The old man tossed her luggage down and gave her a quick wave. "Name's Jesse. Call me if you need me." And he drove off.

"Great!" fumed Codie. "What if Miss Oldham doesn't have a room for me?"

Miss Oldham, a stout, erect woman of indeterminable age, had a nice room for her: one flight up near the front. Codie thanked her.

"You're welcome, Miss Merideth," said Miss Oldham. "You seem familiar to me. Ever stayed at my place before?"

"No, but I worked for a while at Rock Creek Community Center."

"You were an assistant or something, as I recall."

"Youth Director."

"Right. Well . . . enjoy your stay. Bathroom's down the hall. If you don't get any water, just kick the pipes. Sometimes the pump doesn't want to work. Let me know if there is anything I can do for you."

"Thanks again, Miss Oldham. I'll be fine."

Codie unpacked, changed into jeans and boots, then went downstairs where Miss Oldham sat in the front room referred to as The Parlor.

"All settled in?" asked Miss Oldham.

"Pretty much. I was hoping I could find a place to get a bite to eat."

"Oh my, child, not at this hour. You should remember, everything closes early around here. I'll just whip you up something."

"I couldn't ask you to do that," Codie argued weakly.

In minutes Miss Oldham had filled a plate with cold chicken, peas and biscuits, and poured coffee into a fat, heavy mug.

"Um," offered Codie after the first bite. "This is very good. I was famished."

"Staying long here, Miss Merideth?"

"Please, call me Codie. I'm sure I'll be here for quite a while. I want to look for a job."

"What kind of work are you looking for?"

"I'm not too picky. I have to start earning money as soon as possible."

"Well, let me check around in the morning. Might be able to find something for you."

Codie was too tired to argue. Any Job, even one Miss Oldham might find, would be welcome.

★ ★ ★

Morning arrived in filtered rays through the lace curtains, tracing soft light across Codie's bed. She rolled out of bed and walked briskly down the hall to the bathroom.

When she returned to her room, Miss Oldham was waiting, a laden tray in her wide, work-scarred hands.

"You missed breakfast with the other boarders, Codie. From now on, if you're not in the dining room on time, you miss out."

"You're very thoughtful. Thank you. I promise to be more alert from now on."

The town was bustling with early-morning activity. Codie strolled along the main street. Only three businesses held any promise, but one after the other told her, "We aren't hiring right now. Sorry." By lunchtime, Codie was not only tired, but totally discouraged. The afternoon yielded nothing. By suppertime, she felt she had traipsed a hundred miles — all to no avail. When Miss Oldham heard about Codie's day, she clucked her tongue and shook her head.

"Don't you worry, Codie. Now, why don't you help me carry these bowls to the dining room."

The other guests were already at the table. Codie glanced around the table, acknowledging everyone's presence. When her eyes fell on the man who sat at the far end, she gasped.

"Richard?" she cried. "I can't believe it . . . Richard Arlan!"

The man stood so suddenly his chair tipped over. "Codie! What are *you* doing here?"

Codie walked around the table. "Right now I'm helping Miss Oldham. What are *you* doing here?"

"Didn't like Colorado. Too cold and much too far from the Ozarks."

Richard spread his arms wide, inviting her into a warm, welcome hug. Codie rushed to him, startled at how clearly she remembered the comfort he could offer with his burly gentleness.

"It's so good to see a familiar face," Codie said as Richard pulled out a chair for her. "I didn't know I'd feel like a stranger when I came back."

"Why did you come beck?" he asked. "Not that I'm complaining!"

Codie held his gaze, remembering those green-flecked eyes and that flaming red hair, feeling secure in the knowledge that here was someone who understood her, someone who would be there if she needed him.

"You didn't like Colorado," she answered. "I didn't like the big city."

"Where's Marlena?"

"Europe."

The others who sat at the table gawked in open fascination. Codie elaborated on Marlena's exciting European assignment. Even Richard was impressed.

The conversation between Codie and Richard absorbed everyone completely. When dessert and coffee had been finished, nobody made a move to leave the table. Finally, Richard stood.

"How about a drive, Codie? We'll go by Rock Creek, take a look at the new dam . . . get you reacquainted with your surroundings."

Codie hurried upstairs for her jacket. When she came down, Richard was waiting out front, seated in a tan and brown four-wheel drive Wagoneer.

For a while they rode in silence, passing familiar sights that rushed through Codie's memory. She exclaimed excitedly as each new scene came into view. At last they reached the Rock Creek Center, high on a knobby hill. Richard steered the Wagoneer up the narrow red-dirt road and stopped.

"Well, there it is. Look any different?"

"Not at all," Codie sighed. "I understand someone has my job."

"Guy named Anderson. He's pretty good, they tell me."

"It figures. I blew my chance to make a mark in history. The first woman Youth Director at Rock Creek. It was some kind of a mark."

Richard started the engine again. "I'm glad you're here, Codie," he said as he spun the wheel around to start back down the road. "Real glad."

★ ★ ★

When several days had passed and Codie had not found a job, she began to fear she had made a terrible mistake leaving the city. At least there she had an income.

At the end of the first week, she began seriously to consider returning to the university and mentioned her intent to Richard.

"No, Codie, no! I won't let you."

79

"But I can't find work, Richard. I cannot live on nothing."

"We'll find something. Please, give it a few more days."

"Okay, one more week. But that's it."

He smiled broadly and hugged her. "Good girl."

7

AT last Codie was offered a job — thanks to Miss Oldham. She was to begin work immediately as a salesclerk at Rider's Dulcimer Shoppe. When she saw the beautiful instruments, she knew she could sell them. The smooth, polished wood, so perfectly handcrafted into sleek musical boxes with long necks, shone in magnificent splendour. Her fingers touched the strings, bringing forth tones of such clarity she caught her breath.

"Like it?" asked Carl Rider, her new boss and Miss Oldham's nephew.

"Beautiful," sighed Codie. "You must be very proud of what you do."

"Some days, when everything goes just right, I feel there is nothing better in the world."

"That must be wonderful." Codie began counting coins into the antique cash register. In a few minutes, the doors would open for business.

Her mind seemed to have locked itself on her plight. What was she doing selling dulcimers in a tiny shop? A dream formed vivid pictures in her head as she worked: large, high-ceilinged building with lots of windows. Children everywhere, laughing, playing, bringing her their child-size problems. Children who, for one sad reason or another, did not have a place to be themselves, a place where they could find the love and attention they so sorely needed.

The days passed swiftly as Codie sold the beautiful dulcimers and, during the slow times, listened to Carl strumming and singing haunting songs of the hills. On occasion he would teach her a few chords and her fingers would tingle from the vibration.

Richard was with her as much as his job as forester would allow, driving her to the shoppe early in the morning and picking her up when it closed.

Codie accepted his solicitation willingly, unaware it was rekindling in him the love they had once shared.

★ ★ ★

Codie and Richard had met during a week-long retreat far back in the hills where tents were staked out and campfires were built. They each had gone as a sponsor for the youth — Codie from Rock Creek; Richard from South Bend. At week's end their friendship was as stable as the tall trees that shaded their campsite. It was only when Richard asked her to marry him that she realized she did not share his intensity of affection. Not long after that, Richard moved to Colorado. Codie was never sure if she was to blame for his leaving.

Now, once again, she accepted the uncomplicated relationship, being with Richard whenever she could, not asking anything of him — not giving anything of herself.

When Codie had been at the shoppe for nearly a month, Carl rewarded her by offering her an extra day off. Little did she know that he and Richard had conspired to get her away from the shoppe for a day.

"Well," Richard said excitedly when she told him, "we'll have to make big plans. How about driving over to the caverns? We can take a lunch . . . "

His green eyes snapped so brightly with excitement, they gave away his secret. Codie laughed and punched him lightly on the arm.

"Okay, Richard. How did you talk Carl into letting me off for the day?"

"Just a little persuasion," Richard admitted. "Told him I thought he was a slave driver."

"You didn't!"

"He bought it. Let's not question it."

The drive to the caverns was even more beautiful than Codie had remembered. Trees stood limb-to-limb on both sides of the winding road, casting long, cool shadows over the Wagoneer. When they reached their destination, they walked to the gift shop and cafe that served also as the entrance to the caverns. They checked the schedule and found they had just missed a tour.

"How about coffee?" asked Richard.

After giving their order to the waitress, they sat looking out on the expanse of green, sloping mountains. It seemed to draw Codie into its isolation.

"Does anyone live up in those hills?" she asked.

"If they do, no one has ever seen them. It's pretty rough up there. Nothing but rocks and steep inclines."

"But it looks so peaceful from here. Harmless."

"Yeah, well, looks can be deceiving. The danger lies in not knowing what you're getting into. Once you're in there, you have to fight your way out, and not everyone can do that."

Codie lowered her eyes to cover the

sensation that passed through her: the feeling of total abandonment, of not being able to fight her way out. She had allowed herself to be lulled into a life of helplessness, being cared for, guided by those around her. Instead of serving, she was being served. She was without spirit. It was all so easy.

"Codie?"

Richard was leaning across the table, holding her hand.

"Codie? You all right?"

"Yes."

"You seemed to leave me there for a minute."

"Sorry."

The waitress set their coffee on the table, sloshing some of it into the saucers. Codie lifted her cup and patted paper napkins into the dark liquid.

"Codie, where were you just now?"

"Right here," she smiled, hoping to put a stop to his questioning.

"No, you weren't. Is it anyone I know?"

"Who?"

"The man who has hold of you."

"Don't be silly." She clasped her hands in her lap, not wanting Richard to see how they shook.

"Don't you think I know? He's with us all the time, between us. How bad is it, Codie?"

"Please, Richard, there isn't anyone."

"In that case . . . " he put a rough, strong hand against her cheek, "let's talk about you and me."

He could not have accepted her denial so easily. He was trading on her vulnerability, and she was almost willing to let him.

"What about you and me?" she asked.

"You and me. Us. I still love you, Codie. Nothing has changed. Not for me, anyway."

"I've changed, Richard. I'm not the same person you knew before."

"So, I'll get to know the new you. Give me time."

Richard paid for their coffee and they climbed into the Wagoneer. Codie sat stiffly against the seat, uncomfortable under Richard's openly affectionate side-long glances. He put an arm around her, urging her to sit closer to him.

"Please . . . don't," she begged him.

He said, "Sure," and put both his hands on the wheel. "Where shall we eat?" he asked.

Codie had almost forgotten the stuffed wicker basket that sat behind the seat. Miss Oldham had filled it with fried chicken, cheeses, rolls, salad and chocolate brownies. An insulated cooler held ice cold lemonade.

"You're the ranger," she said. "You decide."

Richard steered the four-wheeler around the lake to the edge of a cove hidden from view by trees that hung out over the water. He turned off the engine and got out.

"Coming?" he asked as he picked up the basket and cooler.

Codie slid from the seat and followed him to where he spread out an Army blanket and began taking contents from the basket. She sat on the blanket and watched, amazed at such brawniness dealing so carefully with paper plates and plastic spoons. He handed her a filled plate.

Codie felt no sense of urgency, no pressure to be somewhere else. It was as if her life had been levelled out to an effortless monotone. She sighed and picked up a piece of chicken.

"Oh, here," cried Richard, "you'll get all greasy. Let me wrap that in a napkin."

Codie wiped the grease off her fingers and, when she did, the keen, vivid image of another place slashed into her consciousness, causing unbidden tears to surface. It was as if she could hear Sam's voice: "Don't try to be too neat. Just dig right in."

Richard handed her the piece of chicken, protected with napkins.

"Want to talk about it, Codie?"

"About what?" She kept her eyes averted.

"You are carrying a heavy load. I figure it's a man, and I figure you are still hung up on him."

"I'm not hung up on anyone, Richard."

"I see." He studied her for a while before picking up his own plate. "Miss Oldham sure knows how to put a feast together."

"Yes, she does."

It was a silly conversation, meaningless words spoken so they would not have to deal with what was really on their minds. Richard stretched out on the blanket, resting on one elbow. Codie stared out across the water.

"How long are you going to stay here?" he asked. "I mean in town."

"I have no plans beyond tomorrow," she told him, not knowing it herself until then. "I'll have to find a cheaper room somewhere. As much as I like the dulcimer shoppe, it doesn't give me any sense of accomplishment. I want to find something to do with myself."

Richard turned over on his back.

"Anderson's left Rock Creek."

"What?" Codie moved closer to him. "Don't tease me, Richard."

"I'm not teasing. He was offered a job in Alabama."

"Oh, Richard," she kissed him on the cheek and sat back on her heels. "Why didn't you tell me?"

"I had to know what you wanted before I tried to bribe you with Rock Creek." He was smiling, so obviously pleased with her reaction.

"How long have you known?"

"Only a couple of days. The director called me and asked if I knew of anyone who could take Anderson's place."

She beat both her fists against his thick, muscular arm.

"Richard Arlan! Stop this teasing. What did you tell him?"

"I said I'd give it some thought."

She jumped up and yanked at the blanket. "Come on! Come on! Richard! *Move* it! We're going to Rock Creek."

Laughing heartily, he rolled over

onto the grass and stood, refusing to help her as she gathered everything together.

"If that job is gone, I'll never speak to you again!" she threatened.

"It won't be. Why do you think I asked Carl to give you the day off?"

Inside Rock Creek Community Center, Codie stood in dazed remembrance, relishing the feeling of that memory.

She walked down the centre aisle and turned left to a door marked 'Administrator'. Richard sat on one of the benches to wait for her.

"Mr Fielding?" she spoke as the door swung open at a touch.

"Codie! Come in, come in. It is so good to see you." He took her hand in both his and shook it vigorously.

"Please . . . sit down. Richard told me you were back. We have missed you."

"Thank you. It's good to be . . . home again."

"Are you ready to rejoin the staff?"

"I'd like to. If you need me."

"Oh, we do. Mr Anderson had a better offer, but he had started some very ambitious programmes for the youth here. I hope we can carry them through."

Codie sat back further in her chair and crossed her legs. It seemed so natural to be there.

8

SAM spun the Jaguar around and backed it into the hangar. Dirk opened the car door. "Howdy, Mr Everett. Golden Eagle is all fired up. Randall wants to know if you want him to co-pilot."

"Tell him yes. We'll take off in twenty minutes, if our passengers are here."

Randall came out immediately.

Sam walked out to where the Golden Eagle sat perched on the apron, ready to soar at his command. He had not taken it up since Codie left. Even though the two of them had never flown in Golden Eagle, its very presence reminded him of her. He could still feel the sweet gardenia smell of her cologne in his nostrils, still imagine the sparkling tone of her laugh, the husky whisper of her voice, still sense her closeness as he had kissed her.

He had been so angry with Codie Merideth for leaving West Brook without a word, he had nearly convinced himself she meant nothing to him. Then, when he had learned his secretary had failed to call Codie about his last-minute trip to Alaska, he forgave her. And he missed her. It hadn't been difficult finding out where she had gone. Where else but Rock Creek. A thousand times he had nearly hopped in a plane and gone after her, but then had changed his mind, torn between wanting to be with her and being angry that she could leave so easily. No woman had ever given him so much pleasure, and so much pain, at the same time.

"Sam, ooh-hoo, Sam!" He glanced up to see Bev Sloan and her entourage rushing toward the plane.

"Hello, Bev. We're ready when you are." He lifted a hand and motioned to Randall. They climbed aboard. Sam joined Randall in the cockpit and clamped on his headset. He thought of Codie and how she had stood at the cabin window, looking out over the clouds, asking him what miracle kept the plane in the air.

"You're the wind beneath my wings, Codie, he mused as the plane's nose lifted toward the clouds. Don't you know that?"

★ ★ ★

Codie felt at home in Rock Creek, as if she had never been gone. She still worked part-time at Rider's Dulcimer Shoppe, but most of her time was spent at the centre, carrying on the programmes that Anderson had initiated. She made a few changes but, for the most part, simply expanded on what he had started. She was content, and at times felt a true sense of being useful.

Miss Oldham fretted so about Codie's

need to find a less expensive place to live that they worked out a compromise. She would lower Codie's rent and Codie could help her with dinner and cleanup.

Richard made the suppertime cleanup much easier by sitting in the kitchen talking with her as she worked. When she was finished, they would go for a walk or spend time up on the mountain, under the stars. All was routine. And effortless.

On one such evening they drove to the dam to watch a small two-passenger helicopter as it flew tourists back and forth across the water.

"Cold?" Richard asked.

"A bit."

He slipped an arm around her and pulled her head down to his shoulder. "How was work today?" he asked.

"Okay. I sold two dulcimers to a woman from Rhode Island for her grandsons. Said she wanted them to learn to play and develop a feel for 'the basics', she called it."

"Do you think they will?"

"I doubt it. She's trying to draw them into a time she remembers. You can't transplant a person into another time . . . or another lifestyle."

"Glad to hear you say that," Richard said softly. "I've been wanting to talk to you about that."

"About the woman from Rhode Island?"

"No, Codie, about another lifestyle."

She stiffened against his arm. He felt it and held her even tighter. "Don't fight me, Codie. *Let me say it*. I love you. I want you to stay here. I want you to marry me."

The helicopter soared overhead and dipped toward the water. As it spun back to the opposite shore, Codie longed to sail with it, to rise above where she was, where Richard waited for her answer.

"Codie? Will you marry me?"

"It isn't something I can answer right now, Richard. Give me time."

"How much time? You've been here

nearly three months."

"Yes, I know. But I can't be your wife, Richard, if I'm not sure."

"That's okay. I'm willing to give you time to be sure. But in the meantime, marry me. We'll begin our life together."

She settled even further into the crook of his arm, her eyes closed. What he was offering was so easy. A life of simple integrity, of shared struggles and ambitions. "A few days, Richard, give me a few days."

"Sure." He kissed the top of her head.

They climbed into the Wagoneer. Richard steered it out onto the road and headed west. As they turned onto the main highway, Codie's eye caught a glimpse of a high, dark mass to her right. The bright moon shone down on it like a beacon light.

"Stop!" she cried. "Stop!"

Tyres squealed in rebellion as Richard slammed his foot against the brake.

"What? *What*?" he demanded, looking

about anxiously. Codie was already opening the door. "Codie, where are you going?"

Richard climbed out and followed her as she ran across the ditch and up a small rise. A six-foot high 'For Sale' sign was braced against a dead tree. Richard put a hand on her shoulder and turned her sharply around.

"What in the world is wrong?" he demanded.

"Oh, Richard, look . . . up there." She pointed to a massive hulk of a building standing dark and imposing on the hillside. "That's it! *My building*."

"What do you mean, your building?"

"It's perfect, Richard. That's my . . . " And she knew in that instant what she would call it. "That's my Loving Home."

"Let's get back in the car and see if we can't calm you down. I think you have lost your senses."

Codie followed him back to the Wagoneer. She kept her eye on the moon-drenched building as they eased onto the highway and drove away. "Thanks for stopping, Richard," she said.

"Why did we?"

"I want to make a home, Richard, for children who need love. I want a place where they can come and feel they belong. So many children don't have any place to go. I want to be that place." She was surprised to see a stiff, tight set to his jaw. "What's the matter, don't you think it is a good idea?"

"It may be a good idea," he mumbled," but not for you. What about us, Codie? I want you to be my wife. Let someone else take care of those children. We'll have our own."

* * *

Marlena opened the apartment door and was stunned by the musty, clammy feel. "Codie? You here? Codie?"

She went to the kitchen and her eye

101

caught the letter on the table.

Dear Lenie," it read, *"I hope you had a wonderful stay in Europe. I have gone back to the Ozarks. I took only my half of the savings. The rest is for you. When you get back, drop me a line and I will call you. We will need to talk about the apartment. Love, Codie."*

Marlena stuffed the letter in her pocket. "Why would she do a silly thing like that? And where's Sam?" She picked up the phone to dial Bev Sloan. "Sorry, Marlena," answered the receptionist, "Miss Sloan is out of town."

"When will she be back?"

"Don't know. She's gone to L.A."

"Did she leave any assignments for me?"

"Only one. Neaman's Sportswear."

"I'll get in touch with them tomorrow."

"Talk to you later."

"Uh, Margie, wait. Do you have Sam Everett's home phone number?"

"Just a minute . . . here it is."

Marlena jotted the number on the back of Codie's letter. "Thanks." She dialled Sam's number.

"Mr Everett? Marlena Merideth."

"Well, Marlena, how was Europe?"

"Fantastic, of course. I just got back. Codie isn't here. She's gone to Rock Creek."

"I know."

"Did she say why?"

"I haven't seen Codie since our trip to Chicago."

"What happened?"

"A total breakdown in communication I suspect."

"Want me to tell her to call you?"

"No! No . . . let it be, Marlena."

"If you say so."

"Bev was eager for you to get back. Have you called her?"

"I just did. She's gone to L.A."

"Be sure you catch her when she gets back. She has a big job for you."

"The Neaman thing?"

"Bigger than that."

"Sounds good. If you hear from Codie, let me know."

"I'm sure I won't, Marlena. Goodnight." Sam cradled the phone. It wasn't that far to the Ozarks. He could be there in less than an hour. He had no idea where she was staying. He would just have to wait. The waiting wasn't going to be easy.

★ ★ ★

The youth of Rock Creek and those of South Bend had been planning the campout for weeks. By the time the weekend of the trip arrived, everyone was as wriggly as a can of worms. They met at the centre at six a.m., bleary-eyed but eager.

"When do we start, Miss Merideth, huh, when?"

"Soon. Just hold your horses."

She pulled one of the boys from atop the van that stood next to Richard's four-wheeler. The driver sat behind the wheel scowling. Codie leaned through the window and patted his arm.

"Don't worry, Jesse," she soothed, "it's only for two days."

Jesse smiled at her and winked. "I know."

"Hey, Chuck," Richard yelled, "you and some of the others go back in and get the rest of this stuff."

Codie stepped away from the van, bumping into one of the girls. "Oh, Kristie, sorry. I didn't see you there."

Kristie had been dogging Codie's heels for weeks, begging for affection. She was a lonely child, raised by an elderly grandmother. Codie had been giving her extra attention. Kristie had taken to the attention with a heart-breaking eagerness. She resented anyone being near Codie.

Richard drove the Wagoneer; Codie sat in the seat next to him. Behind them, a carload of youth sang camp songs all the way to the campsite.

With the help of eager hands it took Richard and Jesse twice as long as it should have to set up camp. Codie built a fire and set the large blue-speckled coffee pot to heat. Some of the girls wandered down toward the stream that ran near their site.

Codie kept an eye on them. Mr Fielding took a few of the boys on a wood-hunting trek.

Later Richard called everyone together for opening service: a short Bible reading, a few songs and a circle prayer. Some of the prayers were concise, one-sentence marvels of brevity, but they were offered with a childish sincerity that touched Codie's heart.

That night, by the time supper was over, everyone was exhausted. Codie and Richard sat close to the fire, waiting for it to die out.

"This is much more fun when you're along," said Richard.

"They're like a handful of snakes . . . they keep slipping through your fingers! What's on the agenda for tomorrow?"

"Early morning service; a hike with canteens and backpacks; then a planning session during which they get to tell you and me what we should be doing for them."

"Are you sure we can get all that done in one day?"

"You'll think it's a week's work when you get back from the hike."

"I'm not going hiking."

"You're a sponsor. If you don't go, they'll think you're chicken."

Codie laughed. "I refuse to like it."

Richard kicked dirt over the last embers of the fire. He put out his hand to help her up. "Good-night, chicken," he chuckled, bending to kiss her lightly.

Codie crawled into one of the tents and quietly slipped into her sleeping bag. Kristie, who insisted on sharing the tent with her, was fast asleep. Codie's mind wandered back over the day. It had been exhilarating. She had not been too eager to make the trip when Richard told her they would be going up into the mountains.

"Where we are camping is safe,

easy to get in and out. Besides," he reassured her, "you'll have a ranger with you!"

"Of course," she had teased, "but does this ranger know what he's doing?"

Richard had smiled, "Not all the time." And she knew his reference was not to their choice of a campsite.

9

RAIN beat against the plane in maddening insistence as Sam sat forward in his seat, straining to see through the deluge. Next to him Randall talked with the tower. He turned to Sam.

"Come in on two-niner," he told him. "It's the only one they have."

"I heard. Talk to the passengers. Let them know it could be bumpy."

Sam shot a quick glance at the instruments then began his descent, listening intently to instructions from the tower. The nose of the plane finally broke through the clouds and he had sight of the runway. He heard the comforting hum of the landing gears engaging, but he didn't relax until he felt the wheels touch down. The plane slowed to a smooth stop, just short of the end of the runway. Atlantic City had never looked so good.

Sam taxied the plane to a space near the terminal and shut it down. When he stepped into the cabin to greet his passengers, he was calm and efficient, bearing no hint of the strain he had just endured.

"Nice going, Sam," said Bev Sloan as she stood at the open hatch waiting for the stairs to be rolled into place.

"All in a day's work," he answered.

"Dinner later?" she asked as she stepped out under the protection of a canopy. "I'll be at The Quincy."

Sam nodded.

"Around seven."

Sam and Randall took a cab to their hotel and checked in. Sam was tired. He longed for a long, hot shower and supper in his room. But, he had promised Bev.

Before stepping into the bathroom, he took from his bag a huge towel, 'Nebraska' written across it in red. The towel had arrived in the mail after he and Codie had returned from Chicago.

Apparently she had left it in her room.

Twice he had thrown it away. Twice he had retrieved it. Keeping it served to remind him that Miss Codie Merideth had little regard for him. It was his way of trying to hold his feelings in perspective.

He met Bev in the lobby of The Quincy. She was resplendent in a sequined dress and strappy high-heels.

"Sam! You look smashing," she cooed.

"So do you, Bev. Ready?"

She put a possessive hand on his arm and motioned to the bellman. "My car, please," she ordered. He spoke into the in-house phone then tipped his hat to her.

"Be right up, Miss Sloan."

"Your car?" questioned Sam.

"Rented. Thought we would want to go in style."

It was a luxury car, long and stately, its blackness shining under the lights; a chauffeur dressed in livery sat erect behind the wheel.

"What's this?" frowned Sam.

"I told you — we're going in style. Don't you like it?"

"A bit showy for my tastes," he said.

For Sam the evening dragged. Bev was cloying, clinging to him like sugar-sweet icing on a cake. When, after an agonizingly long dinner, Bev suggested dancing, Sam begged off.

"Now, Sam, don't be an old stick-in-the-mud! Come on, it will be fun."

"Sorry, Bev. I've had a long, rough day."

"Well, what you need is to swing a little, loosen up." She pouted, "I'm not used to being turned down, Sam."

"Look, I'll take a cab back to my hotel. You stay and have a good time." He stood and reached into his pocket.

"No, no, Sam, this is on me."

He threw money on the table. "Oh, no, it's not, Miss Sloan. Good-night."

In long, anxious strides, he left the restaurant, eager to be out in the air, to breathe a little freer. He hailed a cab. "The Bradley," he said and settled back, still angry at Bev for her attempt to 'buy' him. Surely she did not believe that it meant anything to him. Money was only money. It couldn't buy what a man wanted the most.

Oh, Codie, please get out of my life!

But he knew she would always be there. No matter how far away she ran, she would always be a part of him.

* * *

Kristie shook Codie excitedly. "Come on, Miss Merideth, it's time to get up. The rest of the guys are already eating breakfast."

Codie stretched full-length inside her sleeping bag. She could smell the inviting aroma of bacon cooking over an open fire. She looked up at a smiling Kristie. "You go ahead, Honey. I'll be along."

"Oh, no, I want to wait for you."

Codie accepted the girl's hovering and crawled out of her bag. Every bone in her body ached from a night on the hard ground. She wasn't as fond of camping as she used to be.

Following breakfast, Mr Fielding spoke briefly to them about the day's plans, after which boisterous singing from young voices was accompanied by Jesse on a hand-worn dulcimer.

Jesse had agreed to watch the camp while they were gone on their hike, a job Codie coveted with all her heart.

Richard divided the group, putting each adult 'Chief' in charge of seven little 'Indians'. Codie was given the youngest of the children and, of course, Kristie, who had fussed until she was allowed to be with Codie.

They headed out: Richard and his seven; Mr Fielding and his team; and Codie's group bringing up the rear. Codie shifted her backpack and took her place at the tail-end of the procession.

The incline was rough, strewn with

rocks and prickly plant life. Several times Codie had to stop and shake pebbles from her shoes. Her clothes were snagged and her skin itched.

She fell further and further behind, able to keep her eye on her charges only by rushing pell-mell ahead at regular intervals. Following one such surge of energy, she counted heads once more and came up short. She counted again, making note of those she saw.

"Where's Kristie?" she called out anxiously.

Someone ran ahead shouting, "Kristie? Kristie?"

No answer came back to them.

Quickly they lost sight of those who trekked ahead as they stood shouting for Kristie. Only the sounds of the thick foliage answered them. Sharp, cold fear clamped itself in Codie's chest, making it difficult for her to breathe.

"Chuck!" she cried, "go up ahead and tell the others to wait on us. But don't leave my sight, do you understand?"

Chuck nodded, proud of being given such an important task. He eagerly clawed his way upward. In a few minutes, he started back down again.

"I don't see them, Miss Merideth. They're too far ahead."

"Okay . . . okay," Codie stretched the words out to force calmness into her voice. "Now, I want everyone to gather close to me. Who saw Kristie last?"

A small hand went up.

"Becky? When?"

"When we left camp."

That was no help at all. What could have happened to her? Codie turned away from the children for a minute. She was terrified, but had to keep control.

"I think the best thing for us to do is work our way back to camp . . ."

"But what about Kristie?" several cried.

"We are going to look for Kristie on our way down. She has to be somewhere between here and the camp . . . and we'll find her! We will." Codie spoke sternly. "Now, let's form a line. Chuck, you take the lead. Becky, you're next . . . that's it. I'm going to be at the end of the line, so be sure you stay in close ranks."

Codie slipped her arms from the backpack and let it fall to the ground. She couldn't be encumbered with unnecessary weight. Keeping her eye on Chuck to make sure he stayed on the trail, she called out every few steps.

"Kristie! Kristie! Where are you?"

The children chimed in, their voices soon falling into a sing-song rhythm.

God, Codie prayed, please help us find Kristie. Let her hear us call. Show us where she is.

Codie fought the branches that hung across their path. One flew back and slapped her in the face, leaving a burning scratch on her cheek.

"Kristie! Please, Kristie, answer us."

They dared not veer from the trail to search for her. Codie halted the procession.

"Let's be very quiet for a moment. If Kristie answers us, we want to be able to hear her."

"Kristie!!"

There was a rustling up ahead, the sound of someone tramping through the underbrush. Codie rushed forward.

Jesse appeared, swinging a stick against the branches in his path.

"Jesse," sighed Codie. "Did you see Kristie?"

"No. I heard you yelling," he whispered, "Where did you lose her?"

Codie pointed over her shoulder. "Up there. All of a sudden she wasn't with us."

"Okay, now you git on back to camp. I'll take a different path. What's her name again?"

"Kristie."

"Hey, Kristie," he called as he struggled up the hill. "Where are ye, Honey."

Codie led six frightened children to the campsite where they collapsed near the fire. Becky thought to draw water from the cooler for everyone. Codie stood at the outer edge of the site, her eyes trying to see through the trees.

"Can we have something to eat, Miss Merideth?" asked one of the boys.

Codie pulled herself away from her lookout. "Yes, of course. There's fruit and bread in one of the bags."

Her mind taken up for the moment with seeing that everyone was fed, Codie was able to function.

When the children began to fret, she picked up Jesse's dulcimer and slowly thrummed the strings, not creating any particular tune, but developing a pulsing rhythm that seemed to lull them into a momentary quiet. Codie's ear stayed tuned to any sound coming from the mountain.

10

THE Neaman's Sportswear job had taken only two days. Marlena was now ready for the 'big job' Sam had mentioned to her. At first, she had not believed Bev Sloan when she had told her about their next assignment.

"You're joking!" she had gasped over the phone.

"No, Marlena, I'm serious. You will leave for Hawaii on Wednesday. Be prepared to stay at least a month."

Excitedly, she had written a short letter to Codie and packed her bags. Hawaii! She had arrived! No more tiny apartment, no more meatloaf, no more tepid water. She was never again going to do without!

★ ★ ★

In his small office at the end of the hangar, Sam sat with his feet on the desk, the phone cradled against his shoulder. Automatically, he signed cheques his secretary put before him. On cue, he commented, "Um-huh. That's right, Bev. Um-huh."

When she finally got around to the purpose of her call, Sam gestured for his secretary to leave the room.

"You know I can't do that, Bev. I've got one pilot sick, one on vacation. I can't leave right now."

Bev fussed and argued.

"Sorry," Sam said sternly, "you'll just have to go to Hawaii with Marlena and the others. I can't leave right now."

What was Sam's problem? A few weeks in Hawaii with a beautiful woman, sunny beaches and fresh pineapple juice — what more could a man want?

But he knew what he wanted.

It had been three months since he had talked to Codie, ending the conversation in anger when she wouldn't allow him to explain about his trip to Alaska; explain that he had not forgotten her. He regretted having hung up, but he couldn't take it back. He would, he thought, give her time to cool off, then they could rationally discuss everything.

But that time never came. A couple of weeks later, when he had called the university to talk to her, a strange voice answered the phone.

"Miss Merideth doesn't work here any more," the voice said.

"Where did she go?"

"I'm sorry, sir, I don't know," she replied.

It had taken only minutes for Sam to verify that Codie had gone to the Ozarks. It took less than a minute for him to realize that he wanted to be with her.

Suddenly he stood and walked from the office.

"Randall!" he shouted as he ran across the hangar and out to Golden Eagle.

By the time Sam reached the plane, Randall was close behind, shrugging into his Everett Wings jacket.

"We're taking off," said Sam.

"Sure. Where to?"

"The Ozarks. Is the Eagle ready?"

"It's kept ready, Sam, you know that."

Sam pulled himself up into the plane then reached down to help Randall.

"Gee, Sambo," laughed Randall, "who built a fire under you?"

"Close the hatch."

Randall stopped trying to joke with his boss and pulled the heavy door shut.

When Randall entered the cockpit, Sam was already seated, speaking to the tower in crisp, hurried tones as he conducted a pre-flight check.

Randall took his place and waited. When all was ready, Sam turned the plane around and taxied to the runway. Randall never asked any questions.

★ ★ ★

At last, when her nerves had already been worn raw from the waiting, Codie heard sounds of rustling in the underbrush. She ran to the edge of the clearing.

The first to emerge was Mr Fielding carrying Kristie in his arms. She was sobbing, her head resting on his shoulder.

"Oh, Kristie!" cried Codie, rushing to her. She took her from Mr Fielding so she could look at her, make sure she was all right.

"Kristie, you had us so worried. Where were you?"

Kristie turned and pointed back toward the trees where Richard, Jesse and the other children were just coming into view.

"With them?" asked Codie. "But why, Honey? You were supposed to stay with us."

"But you wouldn't talk to me!" pouted Kristie. "You kept letting Becky walk close to you and you held her hand! You're my friend, not hers!"

"Oh, no, Kristie, no." Codie brushed the hair back from the girl's tear-stained face. "I'm your friend, I'm Becky's friend, I'm Chuck's friend . . . "

"No!" shouted Kristie. "You're mine. All mine." She tore from Codie's grasp and ran into the tent. When Codie moved to follow her, a strong hand grabbed her arm.

"Don't, Codie. Let her alone." She turned to see Richard looking at her with dark, brooding eyes. "What's this?" he asked, holding up her backpack.

"My pack. Thanks for bringing it down."

"Why did you leave it, Codie?"

"I needed to hurry. It's only a backpack."

Richard rubbed a hand across his face. "No, it's not just a pack. You scared me half to death! I didn't know what had happened to you!" He threw the bag on the ground.

"Are you all right, Codie? What happened to your cheek?"

"It's nothing. Just a scratch."

"All right. Now, we have to deal with Kristie."

"I know. What are we going to do with her, Richard? What happens when I leave? Who will she have then?"

"The same as the rest of us, I guess," he answered and walked over to the cooler.

Codie watched him. She regretted having left her pack behind, causing Richard to worry. She regretted allowing Kristie to become so attached to her.

And she regretted that she couldn't do anything about any of it. Her helplessness smothered her.

★ ★ ★

Randall watched Sam out of the corner of his eye. His boss's jaw was set in a pulsing tightness that discouraged conversation. Only when they were in the air, did Sam speak.

"Thanks, Randall. For not asking questions."

"Not my place."

Sam chuckled, "It is when you've been shanghaied!"

"You know we're short a couple of pilots, Sam."

"Yeah, I know. We won't be gone long." He pulled off his headset and filled two mugs with coffee and handed one to Randall. "I just have to see if she's all right, Pete."

"I wondered how long it would take you."

"She makes me crazy. I love her one minute, the next I'm so mad at her I could . . . "

★ ★ ★

After the panic over Kristie's disappearance had subsided, no one much wanted to stay in camp. It was agreed they would go back down. A few of the children half-heartedly protested. In the Wagoneer, Kristie reserved a seat next to her for Codie. But, not wanting to endorse Kristie's possessiveness, Codie sat alone causing Kristie to toss her head indignantly and turn her face toward the window. Even though she ached for the distress the young girl suffered, Codie dare not give her further encouragement.

"My, my," clucked Miss Oldham when they told her about Kristie's escapade. "That young 'un needs a good spanking."

"I don't think so, Bertha," argued Jesse. "She needs someone to love her, that's all. That's all any of us needs."

"That's right, Jesse," agreed Richard, "but it doesn't come easy every time." His eyes followed Codie as she poured coffee and set the mugs on the table.

Richard was sitting sideways in his chair, one arm resting on the table. Codie could feel him watching her.

"If you'll excuse me," she began. The jangle of the phone cut her off.

"Codie, would you mind getting that?" asked Miss Oldham.

"I have a person-to-person call for Jesse Wallace," said the operator.

"For you, Jesse." Codie handed the phone across the table.

"Yep," Jesse spoke into the receiver. "Yes, sir . . . an hour or so . . . right." He hung up and stood, downing his coffee in one quick gulp. "Gotta go. Couple of guys landing in Springfield need a lift."

Miss Oldham began clearing away the dishes. "Won't take me a minute. Richard, take her out of here."

He led Codie into The Parlor where they sat together on the sofa.

"Richard, what are we going to do about Kristie?"

"It's more than we can handle. I think we should let Mr Fielding deal with it. Kristie needs more than you can give her."

"Are you saying I don't have the capacity to love?" Codie had no idea why she was suddenly so angry.

"No. I'm saying Kristie is demanding all-or-nothing and she has to realize that's not possible."

Codie pulled herself back into a corner of the sofa.

"I need an answer, Codie."

"I know."

11

SPRINGFIELD tower verified there would be someone to meet them. Sam said thank you and prepared for descent. Never in his life had he gone after a woman. It wasn't his nature to do any pursuing. If a woman didn't want to hang around, that was her privilege, he wasn't going to beg. But now, he was less than forty thousand feet from doing just that. And it made him nervous.

Golden Eagle came in as smooth as a swan on a lake. Randall pulled back the hatch while Sam changed his shirt. He jumped to the ground before anyone could supply steps and crossed the strip in long, anxious strides. Randall called after him, "Hey, Sambo."

"Yeah?" Sam threw over his shoulder.

"When we going back?"

"Don't know."

Randall ran to catch up, panting. "You sure are talkative," he complained.

Inside the small terminal, Sam checked in at the desk. "My ride here yet?" he asked.

"Nope. Be another half hour or so."

Sam paced. First to the window then back again.

Randall extended a foot in front of him.

"You're wearing out the tile, man."

"Sorry. Maybe we should head back to West Brook."

"I think if we do, you'll just be back here tomorrow. Here, drink some coffee."

Sam took the cup, but set it down without taking a drink.

Randall chuckled and sat back to wait.

★ ★ ★

"Codie? Did you hear me?"

"Yes."

Richard had been more than patient,

waiting for her answer. The night they had watched the helicopter passing across the lake, he had asked her to marry him. She had begged time to sort her feelings. Richard had not pressed her. Until now.

"I love you, Codie, but I can't go on waiting. Will you marry me?"

"Things are so easy here, Richard. No pressure, no struggle. It's a comfortable life — basic and good."

"So . . . what are you saying?"

"I'm saying I can't let the . . . the apathy I feel here lull me into making the wrong decision."

"I see!" Richard jumped up and spun to face her. "Is that your answer? That sounds like a no to me."

"Richard, please, wait. I'm just saying I don't know."

"Well," he grumbled, "I know. Good-night, Codie."

For a long while after he left, Codie sat alone, her arms wrapped around her knees as tears slid unchecked down her cheeks.

"Oh, dear Lord, help me," she begged. "What have I done? Richard does not deserve such treatment. Do I love him? Am I fighting what is meant to be?"

Later, after lying awake for what seemed forever, she put on her robe and started down to the kitchen to fix a cup of warm milk. Voices came to her . . . Miss Oldham talking with someone. The voices grew louder; she recognized Jesse's.

"You should have seen that plane, Bertha," he was saying. "Shiniest thing I've ever seen, sittin' there with its bright yellow tail putting all those other crates to shame."

Codie's hand tightened on the railing, squeaking against the polished wood. A fierce pounding laboured against her senses.

The Golden Eagle! It was Sam. It *had* to be. No one else was allowed to fly his plane. Why was he here? She had to know.

Jesse was sitting at the table, a

coffee cup in his hands. Miss Oldham was serving up a generous slab of chocolate cake.

"Why, Codie," she said in surprise, "I thought you had gone to bed."

"Evenin', Codie."

"Who did you bring in from Springfield?" Codie asked.

"Two fellas from West Brook." Jesse sipped noisily from his cup. "Dropped them at the Mountain View Hotel. Said they weren't staying long."

"How long?"

Jesse glanced up at her. "They want to go back in the morning. Why you askin'?"

She turned to leave. "Thanks, Jesse."

Climbing the stairs once again, Codie kept a fist pressed to her stomach. Unbidden, disturbing thoughts of Sam taunted her.

In her room she closed the door and fell across the bed, total exhaustion overtaking her.

What are you doing back in my life, Sam Everett? she begged of the darkness.

The next morning, having slept the night through lying across the bed, Codie stretched against the ache in her muscles.

It didn't matter now. Whatever Sam Everett was doing in the Ozarks, it had nothing to do with her.

★ ★ ★

Sam woke to the piercing ring of the phone. He growled, "Who is it?"

"Sam? You're hard to find."

"Bev! What's going on?"

"Thought you might have changed your mind."

"No, Bev, I have not changed my mind."

"What are you doing in such a God-forsaken place?"

"It's beautiful down here."

"Maybe so. Well? Have you changed your mind about coming to Hawaii?"

"No, Bev. I told you, I'm short of help."

Petulance put an edge in her voice,

"It didn't keep you from traipsing off to another part of the world on a wild goose chase."

"What's that supposed to mean?" Sam was quickly losing patience with Bev Sloan. Even miles and miles away, she seemed to sap his strength with her cloying.

"I know why you're there, Sam. Let her go."

"Good-bye, Bev." Further sleep was out of the question. Was he, as Bev said, being a goose? What kind of idiocy had made him think he could show up on Codie's doorstep and expect her to rush headlong into his arms?

He rolled over and lifted the phone again. "Pete Randall's room, please. Pete, get dressed. We're going back."

"Don't be a sap!" was Randall's sharp reply, "Give her a chance, Sam."

Sam broke the connection but held the phone in his hand.

"What number, please? Hello? Sir? What number?"

Sam put the phone to his ear. "The Bed 'n' Breakfast."

"Bed 'n' Breakfast. This is Miss Oldham."

"Jesse Wallace, please."

"Jesse doesn't live here."

"But we reached him there yesterday."

"You must be one of the men from West Brook . . . Well, Jesse's here a lot, but he lives in a cabin over by the dam."

"Does he have a phone? Do you have his number?" The words were drawn out in tedious impatience.

"Sure." Miss Oldham repeated the number and hung up. Codie came in, still dazed from sleep.

"Morning, Codie. Breakfast isn't quite ready yet. How'd you sleep?"

"So-so . . . what in the world is all over the phone?"

"Oh," chuckled Miss Oldham, "I had a phone call right in the middle of biscuit making."

Codie picked up a damp cloth to wipe away the flour.

"One of the men Jesse brought over from Springfield just called in an awful stew to get hold of Jesse."

Walking as if in a bad dream, Codie took dishes from the cupboard and carried them to the dining room. She placed them around the table and went back for silverware. She would not think of Sam Everett.

The aroma of breakfast soon drew the other guests to the dining-room. Richard was the last one to come in. He glanced at Codie as he sat down. She took a seat across the table and spread her napkin in her lap.

"Codie? I said — would you pass the preserves, please?"

Richard was leaning forward, his steady eyes forcing her to look at him.

"Oh . . . sorry." She handed him the jar.

Codie and Richard spoke only as required and the others, sensitive to the tension, sat in silence. When he finished, Richard pushed back his chair and left the room. Codie heard the front door slam behind him. Miss Oldham rose and motioned toward the kitchen with two sharp nods of her head. Codie followed.

"What's bothering you two?" Miss Oldham wanted to know.

"Nothing."

"Balderdash! I'm not blind. You two had a fuss, didn't you?"

Codie turned on the tap to run hot water into the sink. "The pump's not working again," she said in a lifeless mutter.

"Drats. I'll go down and take a look at it. Sometimes it just needs a swift kick." Before she could cross the room, the phone rang.

Miss Oldham picked up the receiver.

Codie switched on the light and descended the creaky plank stairs. In the far corner sat the derelict pump, shuddering erratically. Codie stepped over a clutter of broken jars and trampled boxes and took a stance behind the pump. Water seeped from a break in the connection where a pipe joined the pump.

"I am in no mood to fool with you. I've had a bad day already and my whole world is coming apart, and . . ." Codie felt foolish as she began to cry. She lifted her foot and, with a swing bearing all her discontent, kicked savagely.

The force broke the connection completely and, with one last spastic shudder, the pump jerked sideways, pinning Codie against the wall. Water flooded madly around her as the pipe, free of its mooring, swung crazily. A broken, razor-sharp piece of metal pressed against her stomach. She could feel it teasing her flesh, daring her to move. Slowly, cautiously, she drew in a long breath to cry for help. But even that slight movement caused the metal to dig deeper into her skin. She could feel the warm flow of blood and knew it had broken through.

"Oh, Dear God, help me, please."

12

CODIE could hear footsteps overhead as someone moved about, unaware that she stood pinned against the rough, dank basement wall, a serrated piece of rusty metal digging into her body. The water, drawn from a spring, grew colder. She dare not move.

The water was rising around her feet. She followed its flow and saw where a soggy piece of cardboard lay over the drain, choking it.

"Okay, Lord," she whispered. "You and I are in a bit of trouble here. I can't get out of here by myself. I'm cold, I'm scared and if I lose consciousness, this pump is going to gouge me. Please, help me. Please."

Suddenly the activity overhead turned to pandemonium. Voices rose in panic. Someone flung open the basement door.

"Codie! Codie!"

She could only whisper, "Here, I'm here."

"Codie! Codie?"

She saw the boots first as he ran down the stairs. He stepped into the water, debris floating around him. She looked up to meet his eyes, but she couldn't see him. Senseless euphoria threatened to steal her consciousness. She couldn't let him move the pump.

"Codie, oh, dear Lord, Codie."

He put his hands against the pump.

"Don't!" she whispered hoarsely. "Don't move . . ."

"Take it easy. I'll get this off you."

"No! Can't move it . . ." She lowered her eyes to where the metal dug into her stomach. His eyes followed.

"Oh, God, please help us!" he cried. "Jesse, come here!"

Codie heard someone step off the stairs. The flow of water was shut off.

"Jesse," he said, "I want you to work your hand under that piece of metal," he said.

"Okay, Mr Everett."

Jesse waded through the water and put a hand to Codie's shoulder.

Codie felt his hand move down her ribs to where the blood trickled from the wound. He pressed in against her stomach, allowing space for his fingers to wedge between her and the broken connection. Once he had the sharp metal covered, he yelled.

"Okay! Push!"

And with one savage thrust, Sam forced the pump away from her.

Codie felt his arms tighten around her as she slipped into blessed oblivion.

★ ★ ★

Sounds wove in and out of her mind like floating clouds. She wanted to raise her hand, but couldn't. She willed her eyes to open. They fluttered then closed again.

"Miss Merideth? Can you hear me?"

Codie turned her head toward the sound. She opened her eyes.

144

A white-clad figure stood beside her. Cool fingers held her wrist.

"Miss Merideth? Can you hear me?"

Codie moved her head up and down.

"Good. How do you feel?"

She closed her eyes again and tried to shake her head.

"You're going to be fine. I'll get Dr Stacey."

Codie desperately wanted to sink back into unconsciousness. She breathed deeply and felt the burning stab of pain just below her ribs. She touched a hand to it, feeling the soft covering. A man's voice roused her.

"Well, you're awake. That's good. Can you look at me?"

With some effort, Codie forced her eyes open. The doctor smiled as he held a stethoscope to her chest.

"You had one harrowing experience," he said as he moved the instrument, listening intently.

Codie ran her tongue over her lips. "Yes," she managed in a husky, unsteady whisper.

"You're going to be fine. Now, I'll tell your friends you are awake. They've been here all day."

"How long . . . " She moistened her lips again. "How long have I been here?"

He glanced at his watch. "Eight hours or so," he said and left.

She looked about the room, taking in its drab, yellowed walls and sparse furnishings. On the table by her bed was a glass and a pitcher of water. She made an effort to reach it, but the movement aggravated her wound.

"Maybe you shouldn't move."

Codie glanced toward the door and the voice. Jesse stood timidly. One hand was bound in a white bandage.

"Oh, Jesse," she cried, "you're hurt."

"It's nothing." He took a step or two forward. "How you doin'?"

"I'm sore. I've got a bandage, so I must be cut or something."

"Or something. You came close to being gored by that connection, Codie. Seems you had someone lookin' over you."

He was almost to the bed now "Uh, I . . . we're sure glad you're okay." He put his bandaged hand against her cheek. Suddenly, he bent and kissed her then stood erect, embarrassed by his action. Codie smiled.

"Thank you, Jesse. If it hadn't been for you . . ."

"And," 'course, Sam."

"Yes, Sam." She looked toward the door.

"Oh, he's not here."

Jesse was hardly out the door before Miss Oldham came bustling in, cluck-clucking in consternation.

"My, my, Codie, you scared us half to death." She put a hand to Codie's forehead. "Are you sure you're all right?"

"I'll be fine. There's a terrible mess in your basement, I'm afraid."

"No matter. And don't you fret about it. Can I get you anything?"

"Oh, water, please. I'm so dry."

Miss Oldham fussed about, pouring water and making sure it was held where Codie wanted it. Codie sipped carefully, unsure how much her unstable stomach would tolerate. The cold wetness soothed her throat.

"I packed some things for you," Miss Oldham said, indicating a small bag she had set on a chair.

"That was very thoughtful."

"No more than . . . " Her eyes brimmed with tears. "No more than . . . Oh, Codie!" She lowered a cheek to Codie's, pressing it gently. "I'm so sorry, Honey. It's all my fault!"

"No, no!" Codie struggled to reassure her. "It isn't your fault. I'm the one who kicked the pump."

Miss Oldham stood and smoothed the covers with trembling, anxious fingers. "You get better now, you hear?" she sniffed.

"I will. The doctor said you've been here all day. Why don't you go home now. I'm going to be all right."

Left alone, Codie relaxed into the soft pillow and mentally surveyed her body. The wound beneath her ribs hurt the most, of course. She could feel bruises here and there. Her feet ached miserably, no doubt from standing in wet boots for so long. And her head was throbbing maniacally.

Through the evening, Codie slipped in and out of sleep, stirring each time she woke to find a more comfortable position.

Sometime around nine o'clock, a nurse brought medication. Codie swallowed it willingly, knowing it would ease the sharp edge of her pain. As she surrendered to sleep, she clung to visions of Sam.

He had not come to see her.

★ ★ ★

Codie awoke, wondering for a moment where she was and why every inch of her body hurt. Recognition came in stages until she was fully aware . . . and grateful to be there. Her first clear thought was of Sam.

He had been so close to her and now

he was gone. She had felt his arms lift her from the cold water and she had clung to him as she was lost to the darkness. Now his absence infuriated her. Tortured her.

Where was Richard? Had she so angered him that he refused to come and see her?

Richard Arlan was as decent and caring as anyone she had ever known. He was a stable, hard-working man who thought first of others, seldom of himself. And he loved her. He had offered her a life with him. An untroubled life of service, of usefulness. A life without complications. What was so difficult about saying yes?

A nurse came to help Codie freshen up for breakfast. It was determined that — if she moved carefully and if the nurse supported her — Codie should try walking to the bathroom. She sat for a moment, dangling her feet over the edge of the bed. She breathed deeply. The room settled.

Codie was glad to get back to her

bed where she sat propped against pillows, awaiting breakfast. She was beginning to suffer pangs of hunger.

But, before her tray was brought in, Dr Stacey entered, studying a chart he carried in his clean, well-manicured hands. A nurse followed close behind, bearing a medical tray.

"Good morning, Miss Merideth," he smiled. "Glad to see you so alert. Hungry?"

Codie nodded.

"Good. They'll be in with breakfast in just a minute. I want to take a look under that bandage."

The doctor's hands were swift and efficient as he peeled back the bandage. Codie shivered involuntarily as he touched the sensitive area beneath.

"Looks good." He spoke to the nurse, "Continue the medication. We don't want any infection. That pipe must have been pretty rusty."

"How many stitches do I have?" Codie asked.

"Looks like fifteen or twenty."

"That doesn't seem too bad."

"You're lucky, Miss Merideth. I can see marks where the metal touched your skin but didn't break through. It could have been a lot worse."

When the nurse and doctor had gone, Codie lifted her eyes to stare at the ceiling. What was happening to her?

Her pondering was interrupted by the arrival of a nurse's aide bearing a breakfast tray. The welcome aroma settled into Codie's senses causing her to sigh.

"Clean your plate, now," the aide ordered as she left the room.

No worry there, thought Codie, I'm famished. She managed to eat only a small portion of the scrambled eggs and one piece of toast. She did, however, drink all of the hot tea. When she had finished she leaned back against the pillows. She hated being so lifeless.

She sank further into the comfort of the bed. The steady swush-swush of soft-soled shoes travelled along the hall as nurses, doctors and aides went about their duties.

Then, in discord to the muffled sounds, came the sharp tread of hard soles, marking each long stride with a confident report. Even before he turned to enter her room, Codie knew he was there.

"Hello, Sam," she said steadily.

He tossed his Stetson onto the chair, covering the bag Miss Oldham had brought.

"Codie . . . " He stood beside her bed, taking one of her hands in his, rubbing it gently. "You scared the life right out of me, did you know that?"

"Thank you for rescuing me."

Letting her hand drop, he hooked his thumbs in his belt and scowled at her. "Hey, what's wrong?"

"Wrong?"

"I'm getting a distinct cold shoulder here. Want to tell me what's bothering you?"

Codie turned her face away from him. If she looked at him, drank in the blueness of his eyes, saw his unruly hair falling over his forehead, she would not be able to hold her reserve. Beneath the covers, she lay tense and unyielding.

"Nothing is bothering me," she assured him.

"Come on," he put a hand beneath her chin and turned her to face him. "What's up?"

She chewed at her parched lower lip. "You couldn't have been too concerned."

"What's that supposed to mean?"

"You weren't here . . . "

"When? Last night? Is that what has you so fired up? Well, Miss Merideth, I'll tell you where . . . "

"It doesn't master," she snapped.

"Yes, it does matter. And you're going to listen." Sitting down, he put a firm hand on her shoulder.

"Your friend Richard and I spent yesterday and most of last night fixing Miss Oldham's pump and cleaning up the basement. Jesse and Miss Oldham stayed here with you. I knew every minute how you were doing."

"But, you didn't come . . . "

"No. I didn't come. We couldn't leave the Bed 'n' Breakfast without water. Someone had to get things back in order." He lowered his eyes. "I'm sorry if you thought I was neglecting you, Codie. I felt needed in so many places. Forgive me."

With that he stood and picked up his hat. "Take care of yourself, Codie. Good-bye."

13

JESSE came to see her later bringing a letter from Marlena.

"Well, I'll let you be. Glad to see you so perky."

"'Bye, Jesse. Thanks."

Codie eagerly ripped open the envelope. There were only a few lines written in a hurried scrawl.

"*Dear Codie: I've gone to Hawaii! Can you believe it? Will be back in a month or so. We can talk about the apartment then.*"

No! Oh, Marlena, how could you? I cannot afford to keep that apartment any longer.

Angrily, she crumpled the letter and tossed it toward the wastebasket. What could she do? She was barely able to pay for her room at Miss Oldham's; she could not work for at least a week, maybe longer; her hospital bill was bound to be exorbitant.

And Marlena had flown to Hawaii without a thought to how Codie was going to manage. She did not hear Richard enter.

"Codie?"

She hurriedly wiped her eyes and turned to smile at him.

"Oh, Richard. I'm glad to see you."

"And I'm glad to see you. What's wrong? The doctor said you're going to be all right, didn't he?"

She nodded. "I'm fine."

"Then, why the tears?" He sat on the edge of the bed. "Don't tell me. Everett was here." His hand slowly dropped to his knee. Hurt etched deep creases in his forehead. "Is that it, Codie?"

"Yes, he was here. No, that's not what is bothering me."

"Then what? Come on, tell me. I'll try to fix it."

"I'm afraid you can't, Richard. But thanks for offering."

"Well . . . if that's the way you want

it. So, when do you think the doctor will let you leave?"

"I hope by the end of the week. I can't afford to stay any longer than is absolutely necessary."

"Codie . . . I apologize for not being there when you needed me."

"You didn't know I was going to do anything stupid, Richard. Neither did I, in fact."

For a long moment he looked at her. "Well, I have to get going." He kissed her lightly on the cheek, no doubt still feeling the tension between them. "I'll be back tonight."

A nurse entered the room carrying a breathtakingly beautiful flower arrangement.

"Sam Everett strikes again," mumbled Richard sourly as he left without looking back.

"Someone sure is fond of you," the nurse said, handing her the tiny envelope that had been pinned to one of the stems. Codie waited until she was alone before removing the card.

"Codie . . . Smell the flowers . . . Fly on the wings of an eagle . . . Sam."

★ ★ ★

Codie was finally discharged from the hospital. She waited for Richard to come for her. That morning she had stood in a shower for the first time since the accident and she still tingled from the sheer joy of its pulsing stream of water on her bed-worn body. She had shampooed her hair and it now framed her face in soft, shining auburn curls. She felt almost human.

Richard held out his arm. "Maybe you better hold on to me."

They left the hospital, stepping out into the bright, glaring sun. Gingerly Codie walked beside Richard to the Wagoneer.

"We don't want any stitches popping loose. Here . . . step on my hands." Richard locked his fingers together forming a stirrup. Codie put one foot in his hands and pushed up with the other, sliding easily onto the seat.

He drove to Miss Oldham's at a snail's pace, concerned that even the slightest bump would cause Codie discomfort.

Miss Oldham waited in the doorway for them, her hands twisted into the folds of her apron. Jesse sat on the porch step, resting against the post. Codie succumbed to their solicitous doting, knowing that to argue would be pointless.

* * *

Back in West Brook, Everett Wings jets flew in and out of the airport daily. Sam dispatched planes with the efficiency of a master juggler. It occupied his time and his mind, but not his heart.

He had called the Ozark hospital twice a day, checking on Codie's condition. He felt confident Miss Oldham would see to her care. When Bev Sloan called again asking him to join her in Hawaii, he could conjure up no more excuses. Bev met him at the Honolulu airport.

She led him outside where a stretch limo waited at the kerb. A chauffeur stood at attention by the open car door.

"Really, Bev, . . . "

"Now, Sam, let me indulge you."

And he did. For three days he allowed himself to be pampered. Bev immersed herself completely in overzealous pandering. Then Sam ran into Marlena in the hotel lobby. She stared in disbelief. "Mr Everett? I didn't know you were here! Did you come down to see Bev?"

Sam had come because Bev had pestered him to do so. He had come in an effort to leave something behind, not to find something.

"More or less," he finally replied. "How's the work going?"

"Fantastic. I hope it lasts forever. Of course, I don't think Codie would like that. We still have the apartment and the rent is adding up with no one living there. I should have talked to her about it before I left, but I was just so excited about coming here . . . " She tossed her head in careless disregard, " . . . Oh, well, she'll manage. She always does." She waved a quick good-bye.

Sam turned sharply toward the front desk.

"My bill, please. I'm checking out." He wrote a quick note to Bev and asked the clerk to slip it into her box. Two hours later he was over the waters of the Pacific.

Randall was only mildly surprised when Sam walked into the hangar late the next day.

"What are you doing back so soon?"

"There's something I have to do."

Sam climbed into the Jaguar and backed it out of the hangar.

★ ★ ★

Codie's recuperation took longer than she wanted. At long last, the doctor gave her permission to resume her job. Richard seemed reconciled to her indecision about their relationship. He was as attentive as ever, making sure she had transportation back and forth each day, and talking with her each evening as she helped Miss Oldham with the cleanup. There was no question about it: Miss Oldham was fond of Richard Arlan and had chastised Codie for not being more receptive to his proposal. Codie could not explain to Miss Oldham — nor to herself — just how she felt about Richard.

He loved her. Not for a minute did Codie doubt that. And he was as staunch a friend as was ever made. Any woman who would carelessly disregard those things about Richard was a fool.

Codie felt like a fool.

"I'm going over to Springfield next week for a couple of days," he told her one evening as they enjoyed a lazy, moonlit stroll.

"Are you?" answered Codie. "I didn't know rangers ever went on business trips."

"Sure we do." He wrapped an arm around her shoulders. "There's a seminar on fire-fighting. I want you to go with me, Codie."

She stopped and pulled away from him. "I can't do that." "I have a job. Two in fact."

"I know that," his voice took on an edge of annoyance. "I'm sure we can work out some time off. It's just for two days, Codie. It's not like I'm asking you to run away with me."

He jammed his hands into his pockets and started walking again, quickly leaving Codie behind. She knew she had, once again, hurt him. She rushed to catch him.

"I'll go, Richard, if you still want me."

14

CODIE phoned the landlord of the apartment in West Brook. She and Marlena still had belongings in the apartment, but she had to eliminate the expense as soon as possible.

"This is Codie Merideth," she told the landlord. "I'm calling about our apartment."

"Yeah." His gruffness was apparent even long distance. "Are you coming back or what?"

"I don't know. But I can't afford to keep paying rent on it. I'm giving notice."

"What for?"

"So I don't have to pay rent."

"It's been paid for six months. Thought you knew that."

"How could I know that?" She pressed fingertips to her temple, wanting to stop the disjointed thoughts that jabbed at her.

"It's your apartment. I figured you'd know any man that would want to come in and plop down that kind of cash for your rent." His vulgar laugh made Codie grit her teeth.

"What man?"

"Ah, come on, lady. The cowboy came in and paid your rent."

Codie let the phone slip from her hand into its cradle.

Sam. Oh, Sam. I can't repay you. I treat you so shabbily, and yet . . . Can you forgive me? What is it with us that we can't ever seem to fly in the same direction.

Feeling as if a yoke had been lifted from her shoulders, Codie went up to her room to finish getting ready for work. Later, as she waited for Richard, she reassessed her dwindling bank account. With the burden of the apartment removed, she could look with some ray of hope at the possibility of paying off her hospital bill, which could take months. Her shoulders drooped in disheartened acceptance. She was going to have to stay in the Ozarks forever.

And with that insight came the realization that the Ozarks meant Richard Arlan, not Sam Everett. It meant there would be no place in her life for posh Chicago hotels or flying above the clouds. She could stop and smell the flowers, but she would never again ride on the wings of an eagle.

On the morning they were to leave for Springfield, Richard knocked at her door long before her alarm went off.

"Hurry up, lazy bones," he called. "We leave at six a.m."

Following breakfast, Miss Oldham insisted on packing a lunch for them. Richard made a big show of trying to lift the heavy basket.

"We're going for only two days," he told her. "Not a month."

Miss Oldham chuckled affectionately. She walked as far as the porch with them, waving as they drove off. Her look of total approval was not lost on Codie.

It seemed everyone thought she belonged with Richard.

They arrived at the south Springfield city limits and fought their way north, through the traffic on Glenstone Boulevard, to Balding Inn.

Richard parked near the front entrance and ran inside for the keys to their rooms. Codie watched other rangers, wandering in and out of the motel. Desolation flooded over her, much like the water that had risen in Miss Oldham's basement. Desolation that could not drain from her because she had clogged the passageway. She had shut off all struggle to do otherwise, to be anywhere else. The peace it brought her was hollow.

The next two days were spent sitting with Richard in high-ceilinged, smoke-filled rooms listening to one lecture after another, breaking only for lunch and an occasional cup of coffee.

An election was held to replace the

incumbent regional director. Richard's name was included on the list of nominees. When the votes were counted, he was the new director. Beaming, he walked to the podium to shake hands with the out-going officer and to accept the gavel of office.

When he returned to his place at the table, Codie put a hand on his arm. "Congratulations, Richard. It's going to be a busy year for you."

He smiled down at her. "But a good year, Codie. We'll make it just fine."

★ ★ ★

Bev Sloan was livid when she read Sam's note. How dare he leave her like that! Well, he wasn't going to get away with it. Whatever it took, she was going to have Sam Everett.

It was several days before a solution came to her. She dialled Marlena's room. "How about lunch?" she asked.

Marlena accepted eagerly.

"How's your sister?" Bev asked with

an air of offhanded concern as they ate.

"Codie? Fine, I guess. Why?"

"Sam tells me she had a terrible accident."

"She did?!" Marlena's fork clattered to her plate. "What happened? He didn't tell me anything about it."

"Oh, my," cooed Bev. "You didn't know? I shouldn't have mentioned it."

Marlena pushed back her chair. "I have to call her. Will you excuse me?" She started across the room, but stopped short and came back to the table.

"I can't," she murmured. "I don't know where she's staying."

Bev reached into her purse and extracted a folded piece of paper. "Here. She's at a place called Miss Oldham's Bed 'n' Breakfast . . . if you can believe that."

"Oh, thank you," Marlena grabbed the note.

Bev smiled sweetly. "You run along and call your sister." And tell her that

Sam was in Hawaii. With me.

It was the next day before Marlena reached Codie.

"Codie?" she cried. "Are you all right?"

"Of course, I'm all right. Why are you calling?"

"Bev said you'd been in an accident? How bad were you hurt? Codie? Answer me."

"I will," laughed Codie, "just as soon as you give me a chance. But first, how did Bev know about it?"

"Sam told her."

"Sam?" Codie pushed a fist against the pit of her stomach.

"He was here. He came down to see Bev. Tell me what happened."

Codie related to her sister what had happened, all the while the cold, hard knot in her stomach twisting tighter and tighter. Sam had flown to Hawaii to be with Bev Sloan. And why not? Bev was from his world. She would never be in awe of plush, swivel chairs in a silver jet, or filmy cream-coloured gowns or big . . . big towels with Nebraska emblazoned across them. She would always be able to pay her rent.

"Oh, Codie," Marlena was crying. "Are you sure you are okay?"

"Yes. I'm fine. When you get back, we'll have to make a decision about the apartment."

"I know. Maybe we can get a bigger place, what do you think?"

"We'll talk about it when you're here," Codie hedged, not wanting to tell Marlena over thousands of miles of phone line that she would not be living in West Brook with her.

Codie put down the phone and climbed the stairs, ignoring Miss Oldham's obvious curiosity. Codie closed the door and turned the heavy upholstered chair to the window. Curling up in its massive comfort, her feet tucked beneath her, she surrendered to the tears she had been harbouring for the past several days.

She loved Sam Everett. Every fibre of her being ached for him. And yet, with her own selfish, stubborn pride, she had spurned his every effort.

Should love be that complicated? Why couldn't it be even-tempered and simple?

Like Richard.

Richard. Was that the love she needed? Was Richard the one to whom she should give her life?

She reached for a tissue and wiped her eyes. She stared out to where the mountain tops met the horizon, and heard again what Richard had said about the hills.

"The danger lies in not knowing what you're getting into," he had said. "Once you're in there, you have to fight your way out . . . "

Fight! Fight, Codie!

15

CODIE tore the sheet of paper from the tablet and wadded it in her fist. She tossed it into the wastebasket where a dozen other balls of discarded stationery lay.

"*Dear Sam: Thank you for your generosity. I understand you have paid the rent on the apartment . . .*"

She began again —

"*Dear Sam: I can smell the flowers, but the eagle has a broken wing. Codie.*"

With deliberate neatness she folded the page and slipped it into an envelope.

"I'm going to the post office," she called out to Miss Oldham.

The short walk afforded Codie time to consider what she was doing. By spreading her feelings before Sam Everett, she was opening her heart to possible rejection. Was she ready to have her life impaled on the shards of a broken heart?

But, if she did not risk it, could she go on, never knowing what might have been?

And Richard, dear Richard.

Codie was forced to accept her decision. She had sent the letter. What happened next was not in her hands. She walked back and found Miss Oldham on the phone.

"Oh!" she said when Codie came in, "here she is now." She held out the phone. "It's for you, Codie. Mr Fielding."

"Codie, glad I caught you. Can you come over to the centre? Kristie's grandmother is here . . . Kristie's run away again."

"Oh, no. I'll be right there." Codie depressed the lever then released it, waiting for a dial tone. "Please be there, Jesse," she whispered as she dialled his number.

"Yeah?"

"Jesse! Codie. Can you run me up to the centre. Kristie's run away again."

"Be right there. Can you find Richard?"

"I don't think so. He's gone over on the other side of the lake."

At the centre, Kristie's grandmother sat hunched forward on one of the benches. Mr Fielding stood talking with her. When he saw Jesse and Codie come in, he motioned to them.

"Makes no difference to me," the old woman was saying. "If she doesn't want to stick around, I can't make her. She's always been ungrateful."

Codie sat down on the bench and reached for the woman's hand. It was given grudgingly.

"Tell me, Mrs Moss, when did you see Kristie last?"

Mrs Moss stabbed a finger toward Mr Fielding. "I already told him. She ate her supper last night and said she was going to go over to her friend's. But she didn't go there."

"Did you and Kristie have a fight?" asked Jesse.

"No! What do you know about it, old man. You've never had any kids."

"Maybe not, but I know what makes 'em hurt."

"Oh? And just what is that?"

"Not being loved. Not belonging anywhere."

Mr Fielding put a hand on Jesse's arm to prevent him from making further comment. "Mrs Moss," he said in a gentle, tempered voice, "Jesse and Codie and I will do what we can to find Kristie. Now, why don't you go on home and wait for us. If Kristie comes back to the house, someone should be there."

"Oh, I'll be there all right," warned the woman as she walked stiffly up the aisle toward the door. "When that little missy comes in, I'll teach her not to run away."

Mr Fielding sighed. "Where do we look first?"

"On the hill," answered Codie with a confidence that seemed to come from somewhere beyond her.

"Good a place as any," agreed Jesse. "We'll take the Jeep. Better get some lanterns, Fielding, and a blanket. If she's been out there since last night, she's going to be wet and cold. That sun may be warm, but it doesn't break through those trees."

The mountain, which had been such a welcome spot for their campout, now seemed foreboding. At the foot of the trail, each of them took a different direction, Codie following the more familiar path. With every step, she called out.

"Kristie! Kristie! It's Codie. Where are you?"

Codie switched on the lantern.

"Kristie!! I love you, Kristie. Please answer me."

From somewhere below her came a sob, a tiny whimper that barely reached her ears.

"Kristie?" She began running down the trail, calling out with every breath. "Kristie?"

Halfway down, hidden by a thorny

blackberry bush, was the lost girl. She sat huddled against the trunk of a tree, her skirt pulled down over her knees, her arms and legs scratched and dirty. Her hair was gnarled and matted around her swollen, tear-streaked face.

Codie sat down beside her and pulled her against her body, willing some of her own warmth to pass to the young girl. She rubbed her hands vigorously on the girl's arms, all the while soothing her with husky whispers.

When Kristie ceased crying, Codie held her at arm's length for a moment and looked her over.

"You don't look too bad," she said. "It does look like you got into something you're allergic to, though. Your face is swollen, but I'm sure . . . "

"I'm bleeding, Codie. I'm bleeding."

"Where? Are you hurt?"

With excruciating embarrassment, Kristie explained it to Codie. Codie pulled her to her again and rocked with her back and forth.

"Oh, Honey, that's nothing to be afraid of. It's just nature's way of preparing you to be a woman."

She stood and helped Kristie to her feet. "After you have had a nice warm bath and a good night's sleep, you and I will talk about it some more."

"Are you mad at me, Codie?"

"No, sweetie, I'm not mad, but a lot of people are so terribly worried. Your grandmother is very upset."

"No, she's not. She doesn't care where I go just so long as I don't bother her."

"I don't think that's true, Kristie. I think she just has a difficult time showing her love . . . "

"You don't."

"No. But I don't always do the right thing with the love I feel. You see, we all make mistakes, and we all need help."

Jesse and Mr Fielding were already at the Jeep. When they saw Kristie, they both let out a loud hoot that echoed against the tree-lined hills above them.

"Well, gentlemen," Codie said, "would you mind seeing the two of us ladies home?"

★ ★ ★

As they came to a stop in front of Mrs Moss' house, Kristie stiffened.

"Can I stay with you tonight, Codie?" she begged.

"No, no. Your grandmother needs you. She may be angry with you, but she loves you. Give her a chance to show it. You do owe her an apology, you know."

"I know. Can I come and see you tomorrow?"

"You bet! Now, run on in."

Kristie wrapped her arms about Codie's neck and held on to her. Then, with a little urging from Codie, stepped out of the Jeep and walked up the steps to where Mrs Moss stood waiting in the doorway.

"That was the hardest thing I've ever had to do," sobbed Codie as they drove away.

At the Bed 'n' Breakfast an anxious Miss Oldham awaited them. Before sitting down to eat, each in turn went up to the bathroom to wash off the mountain dirt. Codie, being last, came down to find Richard waiting for her at the bottom of the stairs.

"Richard! When did you get back."

"Just now. I hear you've had trouble with Kristie again."

"Not trouble. She's growing up, that's all, and it scares her. Mrs Moss has not felt it necessary to explain it to her apparently."

Richard put an arm around her. "Well, I'm glad you're back."

Kristie did not come to see Codie the next day, nor the next. Codie prayed fervently that she had not done the wrong thing by making Kristie stay with her grandmother. On the third day, when she spoke to Mr Fielding of her concern, his only answer was,

"Give it time, Codie. Give it time."

Two letters came for Codie that day: one from the hospital and one from Marlena. She unfolded Marlena's letter, eager to have word of her sister, and not in the least bit eager to see her hospital bill.

"*Dear Codie,*" she read, "*This is going to surprise you — I know it does me! — but believe it. I have met this fabulous man. His name is David Proctor. He has part ownership in pineapple fields here on the islands. He has asked me to stay. I told him I would. Hope everything is okay with you. Love Lenie.*"

"Oh, Marlena," Codie laughed. "Honey, what are you doing? I hope you're happy. Nothing else matters."

Codie put the letter aside and opened the notice from the hospital.

"*Dear Miss Merideth: Enclosed is an itemized statement of your account which shows payment in full. Thank you for your prompt remittance.*"

Prompt remittance! She had not sent

them even one payment. Who then?

Sam.

She tucked both letters in her pocket, her mind wrestling with the sudden turns her life kept taking. Marlena would probably stay in Hawaii. That meant Codie was going to have to clear out the apartment.

And Sam. What in the world was she going to do about Sam?

16

THE letter was waiting on Sam's desk. He glanced at the postmark and felt his heart leap crazily. He put his fingers to the envelope, then pulled them away.

He could not be sure he wanted to know what was in it. Good news he could handle. But what he couldn't deal with was finality, a total breaking away of the relationship that — stormy as it was — they had shared.

With gruff resignation to whatever it held, he tore the flap and pulled out the single sheet.

"Sam: I can smell the flowers, but the eagle has a broken wing. Codie."

"Pete!" Sam yelled. "Fire up Golden Eagle. We're going . . . "

"I know," Randall interrupted with a broad grin, "we're going to the Ozarks."

185

Later, when they had lifted off and the Golden Eagle was sailing smoothly through the cloudless sky, Sam handed the letter to Randall.

Randall scanned the short note.

"Don't you get it?" asked Sam.

"No, Sam, I'm afraid I don't. I don't know what she means by . . . 'the eagle has a . . . '"

"A broken wing! She can't fly without me, Pete." Don't you see?"

"Whatever you say, Sambo."

★ ★ ★

Codie was not at Miss Oldham's when the call came for Jesse to pick up a fare at Springfield airport. She had gone to Mrs Moss' to talk with Kristie. Kristie was not at home. Codie gave up the waiting and went back to the Bed 'n' Breakfast.

Jesse's Jeep, in all its grimy, mud-splattered splendour, sat at the kerb. Codie smiled. She was beginning to suspect that there was more between

Jesse and Miss Oldham than they were admitting.

Her hand was still on the cool, brass knob when she heard his voice — smooth and clear, like water flowing over rocks in a mountain stream. It seemed to fill the house with its music, drifting about her, seeping into her very soul. Her feet seemed to have lost their ability to move.

Then Sam's voice again, rising to meet her like a bird gliding on the wind.

"I'm not moving from this spot until she gets back. How long did you say she'd be gone?"

"Hard to tell," replied Miss Oldham. "Kristie's a handful."

Moving in a lofty dreaminess, Codie glanced in the mirror that hung by the door. Her hair was in wind-blown disarray. She wore no make-up, but her cheeks bloomed a soft pink.

Turning, she walked down the hall. Never had it seemed so long. She put a hand to the kitchen door and pushed it open. She pushed the door wider. First she saw the boots, scuffed and worn, crossed at the ankles as he sat with his long legs extended. Then the faded jeans, tight over his thighs, and above that, the plaid shirt under a brown tweed jacket. On the table lay a white Stetson. She pushed the door all the way back. There was a stillness as if the world had stopped, giving them the moment in which to savour each other.

Sam looked at her, his eyes half-closed, drawing her into their deep bluegreen passion. She lifted a hand to press fingers to her lips, to stifle the cry of joy that wanted so much to escape. He stood, closing the distance between them in easy strides, opening his arms to her. She held her hands out to him, accepting him, wanting only to feel the closeness of him.

When, at last, he brought his arms around her, pulling her against the firmness of his body, she clung to him, her head resting against the warm roughness of his jacket. She could hear the anxious beating of his heart. For a moment they were separated from all that was around them. Codie could sense the feeling — feeling she had tried so hard to shut out of her life — feeling that flowed once again through her body, giving life to the love she had strived so hard to deny.

"Hello, Codie," he whispered against her hair.

She lifted her face to look at him. "Hello, Sam."

He gripped her shoulders and held her away from him, a lop-sided grin teasing the corners of his mouth.

"We're not alone, you know," he teased, as if noticing it for the first time.

Sam reached for his Stetson. "If you're not busy, Miss Merideth," he drawled, "I would enjoy your company for dinner."

Playing his light-hearted game, Codie curtsied. "Thank you, Sir. I would be honoured. How should I dress?"

189

"Spiffy."

"Yes, Sir. What time?"

"One hour."

"Isn't that a little early for dinner?"

"We have a long way to go."

Not wanting to take her eyes off him, she backed through the door. Once it had swung to behind her, she spun quickly and ran up to her room where she pulled garments from the closet and tossed them onto the bed. She finally assembled a flowing challis skirt, a soft, ruffled blouse, and waist-length vest with pearl buttons, all done in muted rust earth tones. She spread them on the bed and dashed down the hall to the bath where she stood under the pulsing hot stream of the shower, feeling her flesh tingle with its pleasure.

At last, she was ready. She walked in stately fashion down the stairs. Sam was waiting, smiling up at her, more handsome than she had ever seen him, in his brightly polished boots, knife-creased jeans and a fleecy light blue

V-neck sweater over a starchy white shirt. He held a narrow tie in his hand.

Codie reached the bottom landing and stopped. Sam reached for her over the expanse of the last three steps. His hands gripped her waist and he lifted her toward him, holding her next to him. She laced her arms around his neck and nuzzled her face in the warm, sweet fragrance of his neck. Then, with a sharp intake of breath, he released her and held up the tie.

"Does this go all right with this sweater?"

"Of course," she answered, reaching up to tie it.

"Not yet," he chuckled. "I don't want to be lassoed until absolutely necessary."

Sam turned to open the door. Just as his hand touched the knob, the door swung open. Kristie burst through, out of breath from running.

"Oh, Codie!" she cried excitedly.

"Can we talk now? Can we?"

Sam was holding Codie's hand in his, the full energy of his love seeping into her very marrow. When Kristie spoke, his fingers tightened as if he were afraid Codie would pull away from him.

"Kristie, I was over to see you today," said Codie. "I was hoping we could have some time this afternoon."

"I have time now," was Kristie's eager answer.

"Oh," offered Codie, "Kristie, this is Mr Everett. Sam, this is Kristie Moss. She and I are . . . " Codie smiled, "friends."

The young girl beamed with pleasure. "Well, can we talk now, Codie?"

Codie fought against the pleading in the girl's eyes. "I'm sorry, Kristie, Sam and I were just leaving. Perhaps tomorrow."

"Oh, please, I want to talk now! I need to talk to you."

Sam's arm tightened around Codie. She could feel the eagerness — and the impatience — in his touch. And she saw the desperation in Kristie's eyes. Her heart ached for the girl's need — and for her own. She looked up at Sam.

"Could we . . . " she began. "It will only take a few minutes."

His arm slipped from her and he stepped back. "Okay, Codie." He did not smile as he walked down the hall and pushed open the kitchen door.

"Now," she said curtly when they were seated in The Parlor, "what did you need to talk to me about?"

Kristie lowered her head, obviously self-conscious under Codie's stern gaze.

"You know . . . you said we could talk about . . . about it . . . "

Understanding flashed across Codie's mind.

"Okay, sweetheart, we'll talk."

Finally, when all of Kristie's questions had been satisfied, Codie hugged her and asked, "Feel better now?"

"Um-hum," murmured Kristie. "It's not easy, being a woman, is it, Codie?"

Codie put a hand to the girl's cheek. "No, Honey, it isn't. But it's worth it. Now, why don't you run along. Sam is waiting for me."

Sam stood at the sink, looking out toward the mountains, working his Stetson back and forth in his hands. She let the door close quietly. He turned, his brow drawn tight.

"I'm ready now," she told him.

"Are you sure?"

"Sam, please . . . it was something I had to do. She needed me."

"I see." He offered a lop-sided smile, not quite ready to accept the delay. "Well, our chariot awaits," he said and moved to hold the door for her. She walked ahead of him down the hall and out the front door.

There at the kerb was Jesse's Jeep, scrubbed clean and polished to glistening new life. Jesse stood in formal attendance near the passenger's side, holding open the door. When Codie approached, he swept low in a grand bow. When he closed the door, she leaned out and kissed him affectionately.

Sam climbed in, extending his legs beneath the wheel.

"Thanks for the buggy, Jesse," he said as he turned the key.

Once they had passed the edge of town, Sam relaxed and gave her a sidelong glance. "I've got you now!" he said.

"What do you mean?"

"No one can demand your attention now. You are mine." He reached for her hand and held onto it as they sped along the highway, the wind quickly disturbing Codie's carefully brushed curls.

"Were you upset?" she asked.

"About Kristie? Just disappointed. I didn't fly all the way down here to be alone."

"She needs a lot of stroking. Her grandmother is elderly. Kristie needs someone she can talk to."

"Well, Kristie has had her time with you. Now it's mine . . . and I intend to make the best of it."

"There are a lot of children like her, Sam. I mean children who need a place where they know they are loved, where they know they belong."

"There are homes like that, you know."

"Yes, but not like mine."

"Yours? I didn't know you had a home for children. Where do you keep it?" His smile seemed to touch her with its gentleness.

"I keep it in my head. I dream about it. It's called 'Loving Home' and it's on a hill with trees all around . . . "

She turned her head toward the window and closed her eyes. Sam's hand touched her hair.

"Hey, Codie, what's up?"

"Sorry. It's just something I want so much. I saw the perfect place the other night. It's a big, sturdy building on the east side of town. It looked so wonderfully inviting with the moon shining down . . . " She took a long, deep breath and gestured as if to erase the whole idea. "Forget it. I'm just rambling on. Now — where are we going for dinner? I hope they don't mind that we're late."

He studied her for a long moment before he answered.

"Dallas. We're going to Dallas for dinner."

"Oh, Sam be serious. Where are we *really* going?"

"We are going to the Springfield airport. We are going to board the Golden Eagle. And we are going to fly to Dallas where we have reservations at Sylvano's."

Codie shook her head in disbelief. "Oh, Sam, Sam. You're crazy, you know that?"

"Maybe." He glanced at her without turning his head, his eyes a warm, deep blue, reaching inside of her.

"By the way, Sam," Codie said after a while, "you wouldn't happen to know how my hospital bill was mysteriously paid in full, would you?"

"I had to do something, Codie. I was

so grateful you were all right. Hope you don't mind."

She rested her head against the back of the seat.

"No, I don't mind. But I'm never going to be able to pay you back — for the hospital, the apartment . . . "

"You already have."

17

THE sun was coming to rest on the horizon by the time they reached Springfield. Randall waited for them inside the small airport terminal. Sam excused himself and walked to the desk where he picked up the phone. His eyes lingered on Codie as he waited for an answer.

"Hi, Dirk," he said into the phone. "Glad I caught you. Yeah . . . send it . . . express mail. Right . . . thanks." He replaced the receiver and took her arm. "Ready?"

She nodded and walked with him out to the Golden Eagle. They climbed aboard. Randall and Jim the co-pilot were already in the cockpit.

"Is he good?" asked Codie as they entered the cabin and took their places in the plush, swivel seats.

"Who? Jim? sure." He took her hand. "Settled?"

"Settled. How about you, Mr Everett? If I remember right, the last time we flew, you chose not to buckle in."

He leaned over and kissed her tenderly, but emphatically. "We're not to mention that," he teased, "remember?"

"I didn't promise not to tease you about it."

"You'll pay!" he chuckled and touched the back of his fingers to her cheek. "You'll pay."

Codie leaned her cheek into the touch, the movement as gentle as a butterfly's wings. Sam caressed the softness of her skin. His fingers opened and slipped to the nape of her neck, clutching it with a suddenness that took Codie's breath away. She closed her eyes and tilted her head against the feeling. She felt his hand on her waist, moving to the small of her back, drawing her to him. His breath seeped inside her as he opened his mouth over hers. She could taste his sweet, clean lips.

* * *

The bright lights of Dallas came into view as they broke through the low, soft clouds. On command from the tower, Randall brought the plane down gently, wheeling it along the runway to a stop.

Sam unfastened his seat belt and reached over to help Codie with hers. She inhaled the fresh, clean smell of his hair and the faint scent of his aftershave. Remembering his kiss, she felt weak, powerless against his very presence.

"We're here. Miss Merideth. Care to join me for dinner?"

"I'm in your hands," she whispered huskily, staggered by her blatantly revealing response.

Randall appeared in the doorway.

"Can I see you for a minute, Sam?" he asked, nodding toward the cockpit.

"Sure." Sam bent and kissed Codie quickly. "Be right back."

While she waited, she strolled to one of the windows and looked out across the airfield, watching small and large craft landing on the paved strips with the grace of dragonflies on a pond. Small wonder that Sam loves flying so, she mused.

Sam emerged from the cockpit. "Well, you tell them I said to fix it," he was saying. When he turned toward her, his sombre expression gave way to a lop-sided smile. "Sorry. Let's get out of here."

"Is there anything wrong?"

"Nothing that can't be fixed . . . Stand back."

Sam stepped onto the stairs then turned to take her hand. Their heels click-clacked on the tile floor as Sam guided her through the terminal to the front entrance where a cab sat waiting at the kerb. The driver opened the door for them.

"Good evening, Mr Everett," he said

as they climbed in.

"Where to?"

"Sylvano's," replied Sam. "And take your time, Frank."

Codie looked from one to the other. "I can't believe you know him!"

"Frank's always here when I need him. We have an arrangement."

"I see, must be nice."

Sam put an arm about her and urged her closer. "Is that a snide remark?"

"No, not at all. I meant it. It must be nice, having such conveniences at your command." She nestled her head to his shoulder.

"Yeah, it's nice, being able to do things for other people that you wouldn't ordinarily be able to do. It's nice having the resources for changing the world for the better, a little bit at a time. It's . . . " he turned his head toward the window. "Sorry. I didn't mean to pontificate like that."

Codie lifted her head and smiled at him. "Never apologize for caring, Sam. It fits you well."

Briefly his lips touched hers — tenderly, affectionately, his breath washing over her, warm and sweet. Holding his gaze, she tugged at the tie that hung unknotted around his neck.

"Want me to tie that now?"

"I guess you might as well."

Expertly she whipped the tie into a perfect knot then tucked the ends inside his sweater. With one last tug at the collar, she said, "There you are. Now, you'll pass inspection."

"Tell me, Miss Merideth," he whispered from deep inside him, "where did you learn to tie a tie like that?" His eyes held hers, their blue depths drawing her closer to him.

"A Youth Director is called upon to do a lot of things," her husky voice was barely audible, quiet and low.

Codie took a comb from her purse and quickly ran it through her curls then flipped them loosely around her face. Sam grinned in appreciation.

The cab pulled into a huge parking lot — past a sign claiming it to be the Turtle Creek Mall — and came to a stop in front of an unobtrusive building. Frank opened the door for them.

"Want me to wait for you, Mr Everett?"

"No, thanks. I'll call when we're ready."

"Sure thing. Evening, Miss Merideth."

"I'm not even going to ask how he knows my name," laughed Codie. "Nothing amazes me tonight."

With his hand resting at the small of her back, Sam led her toward the *maître d'hôtel* who stood, menus in hand, waiting for them.

"Hello, Sam," the man smiled with proper dignity. "Your table is ready."

They wove in and out of the linen-covered tables to a small one secluded in a far corner. In the centre of the table candles flickered in silver holders and a crystal vase held a single pink rose. When they were alone, Codie placed her menu on the table.

"I'm not even going to look at that," she said.

Sam chuckled, "Why not?"

"Because I know the prices are going to be so outlandish I will faint . . . and you don't want that, do you?"

"You can do whatever you want, Codie. But, don't worry. There is no price tonight."

"You mean it's all free? That's wonderful . . . I'll have everything!"

"Sure you will," he murmured, reaching across the table to take her hand. "Everything you want."

Her hand was warm in his, the touch of his fingers sending ripples of pleasure along her flesh.

"I don't have a lot of wants, Sam."

"Well," his voice, too, was held low, "I do. I want you. After that, they get specific." His thumb rubbed the back of her hand. He lowered his eyes, then looked up at her, a half-smile touching his lips. "I want you with me. I want you across the table from me. I want you sitting beside me when I fly. I want you . . . "

A waiter appeared at their table to take their order.

"Hello, Mike," said Sam.

"Good evening, Mr Everett. Are you ready to order now? May I bring you something from the bar?"

"We'll have a bottle of champagne, Mike. And bring us one of those beautiful antipastos."

Mike turned crisply, but not before Codie saw the knowing smile on his face.

"Do you know everyone in Dallas?" she asked.

"No." He reached for her hand again. "I asked Dirk to send something down tomorrow."

"I heard."

"Weren't you curious?"

"It was your business, not mine," she smiled.

"This was your business — and mine."

"Oh? What is it?"

"Not telling," he chuckled. "You'll see tomorrow."

"Then," she jerked her hand away in pretended anger, "why did you bring it up?"

"Because I like to watch what happens to those hazel eyes of yours when something piques your curiosity."

"Am I that transparent?"

"No . . . I'm that interested."

The soft, warm tone of his voice tugged at her.

"Sam," she whispered, "we're so far apart. You live in one world, I live in another. I don't belong . . . "

"Just a minute." He leaned toward her. "You don't belong where?"

"Well, here . . . with . . . " she swept her hand in a wide arc, "all of this. You are comfortable here. I am," she sighed, "I'm awestruck by it all."

"So?"

"So . . . So . . . I don't know. It made sense when I started to say it."

Laughing, he sat erect, putting distance between them. "Oh, Codie, you are so delightful. I . . . "

He stopped as Mike approached, bearing a bottle of champagne nestled in an ice-filled container, and a tray of antipasto.

"We'll order now, Mike," Sam said. "Bring us your special *manicotti* for two."

"Right away, Mr Everett. Anything else?"

"No, that should do it. "But keep two pieces of cheesecake in reserve."

"Now, where were we?" asked Sam.

"You were turning my head, I'm afraid." Codie sighed heavily. "But I won't hold you to anything said on an empty stomach," she laughed.

Sam's brows came together in a sombre show of disapproval.

"Is that what you think? You don't know me very well if you think I throw words like that around."

"You're angry with me."

"You're darn right, I'm angry." He worked his silverware back and forth refusing to look at her.

Codie put a hand on his arm. "Sam, I'm sorry. It's just that I can't seem to bring my life into conjunction with yours."

"You're a snob, Codie. Do you think your world is the only right one?"

"Of course not!"

"The only space between us is what you have created with your own independent isolation. You say you want to serve people, to help. You aren't going to do much of that if you limit your practice to only those people who fit what you define as the 'right life'."

Tears burned behind Codie's eyes, rising from the pain Sam's words caused her. Pain that fed on her realization that what he said bore a truth.

Sam took a long swallow of his champagne. "Do you believe in God, Codie?"

"Of course I do."

"And so do I. What do you think keeps me up in those clouds, Codie?

Air? Wings? Jets? God keeps me up there. He holds me up when nothing else works. He keeps me going when I can't see where I'm going. He brings me down safely when I've given up. I don't go up without Him and I don't come down without Him. He doesn't play favourites, Codie."

"I know that," she whispered, the tears spilling unattended down her cheeks as she held Sam's gaze.

"You want to help people, Codie. Do you think all the needs are in the Ozarks?"

"There is a lot of need there."

"Where you are doesn't matter nearly as much as what you do."

"Sam, why are you doing this?"

"Because I want you with me, but I want all of you, and I know you won't be happy anywhere there isn't a need for you to serve."

She placed a hand on his arm. "Sam, please, forgive me. I have been . . . " she smiled softly through her tears, " . . . a snob."

"Yes, you have." He picked an olive from the antipasto tray and held it out to her. She bit down on it, savouring its tanginess as Sam's fingers lingered on her lips.

18

MIKE had brought their cheesecake, lavishly covered with cherries, and had poured coffee into gold-trimmed white china cups. Sam lifted the rose from the vase and broke the thorns from its long stem. He held it out to her.

"Smell the flowers, Codie," he said.

Sam's hand brushed hers before he let go. She touched the flower to her lips.

"Thank you." She lifted her spoon to take a bit of the cheesecake. It was soft and cool on her tongue. Sam pushed his aside.

"Don't you like it?" she asked.

"I love it. Maybe later." He smiled lazily, his half-closed eyes watching her. "I'm glad you like it."

She glanced up to see Mike approaching, phone in hand.

"Call for you, Mr Everett," he said, handing it to Sam.

"Yes? . . . I don't want to hear that, Pete . . . No! I don't care what they said. I want it ready . . . Well, you make them understand." He hung up.

"What is it, Sam?" Codie asked. "Come on, you can tell me. I'm a big girl."

Surprisingly, he laughed, "That's just the problem. Never mind." His expression of concern deepened. "Just a little trouble with the landing gear, that's all."

"Can they fix it?"

"Sure. It's just taking a lot longer than we expected."

Codie struggled against a rising suspicion. She could not believe Sam would manufacture plane trouble just to keep them overnight in Dallas.

Sam sat straight in his chair, working his cup around in its saucer.

"Tell me about Richard, Codie."

She frowned and clasped her hands together in her lap.

"What about Richard?"

"He's in love with you. Do you love him?"

"I love him because he is a loyal friend and a good person."

"Has he asked you to marry him?"

"How did you know that?"

"It follows. He's in love with you. He wants to marry you. What did you say?"

"I told him I didn't know."

"But you do."

"I suppose. I don't know where I'm expected to be."

"Where you want to be."

"Maybe. Maybe there's another place for me."

"Why do you insist on such vacant denial?"

"Denial is part of life."

"Denial for denial's sake serves no one, Codie."

"You don't understand."

"You bet I don't. What's wrong with planning your life to serve yourself?"

"You don't understand," she whispered.

"Yeah . . . I do." He motioned for Mike. "Check, please," he said solemnly.

"Thank you very much, Mr Everett," Mike said, bowing slightly, "Good evening, Miss Merideth." Codie nodded.

"Mike," Sam asked, "would you call Frank?"

When the waiter had gone, Sam pushed back his chair.

Codie rose, her heart aching under Sam's unsmiling gaze. For a while she had forgotten how diverse their worlds were.

They walked single-file between the tables to the front door where they waited for Frank's cab.

The short ride to Love Field was silent except for Frank's occasional comment. It didn't seem to bother him that no one was responding. At the terminal, he eagerly jumped out and opened the door. Sam slipped money into his hand.

Inside the terminal Sam approached the desk. Codie could not hear the conversation he held with the clerk, but she could see the stiffness come into his shoulders and knew that, whatever was being said, it was not what Sam wanted to hear.

He came back to where she waited. "Let's go," he said, taking her arm and steering her toward the gate. His grip was tight, commanding. Codie bristled under his sternness as she quickened her step to keep up.

The Golden Eagle sat glistening in the moonlight, its jets rumbling in expectation. Sam led her up the steps and into the cabin. Randall emerged from the cockpit.

"Sam, I don't think we . . . "

Turning sharply, Sam motioned him to silence. "Prepare to take off, Randall."

Randall returned to the cockpit, pulling the door shut behind him. Sam closed the hatch.

"Better get buckled in," he said. "I'm going up front."

Codie settled into the cushiony comfort of one of the chairs. Pulling the belt across her lap, she yanked it tight, welcoming the feeling of security it gave her. Outside the window wavy air expelled from the jets. As the plane taxied to the runway, Codie gripped the arms of the chair and wished Sam was there. It seemed to go so much smoother when he was beside her.

The jets roared as the plane accelerated along the concrete pathway to rise, heavy and powerful, into the air. Codie held firm to the chair arms until the plane had levelled off. Then, expelling her breath slowly, she released her belt and leaned back. She never seemed able to separate the intoxicating sensation of lift-off from the anxiety she felt at having left the stability of the earth.

Sam opened the cockpit door and stepped through, bending to clear its low frame. The smile he gave her did not reach his eyes.

"Okay back here?" he asked.

"Fine. Is everything all right?"

"Why do you ask?" He sat down in the chair beside her and turned to face her. Their knees brushed ever so briefly. Codie did not withdraw from the touch.

"Randall seemed concerned earlier," she said.

"Golden Eagle has a limp, that's all."

She smiled. "A limp?"

"The landing gear is a little stubborn."

"Sam . . . " She waited until he was looking directly at her. " . . . why did you allow Golden Eagle to go up when you knew there was a problem?"

"Don't worry, Codie."

"You didn't answer my question."

"Because," he brushed a curl back from her forehead with the tip of his finger, "because I didn't think you would buy another story about aircraft malfunction."

"But, if it's true . . . "

"It's true, but I didn't want you thinking I had come up with another one of my 'lines,' as you called it."

With her face toward him, Codie leaned back against the seat.

"Oh, Sam, how do you have such patience with me?"

"Don't ask me. This is a first. I've never had any reason to try this hard before." He reached for her hand, holding it snuggly in his as the wings of the Golden Eagle skimmed over the clouds. They sat in silence, feeling the pulsing rhythm of the engines; feeling their own hearts beating in unison.

Much too soon, the seat belt signal flashed. Sam gave her a tender kiss on the cheek and snapped her belt in place. As he was pulling his own belt across his lap, Randall appeared at the cockpit door.

"Sam, see you for a minute?" The cold, steady tone of his vice cut fear into Codie's heart.

Sam rose and strode to where Randall waited. "What is it, Pete?" he asked as they entered the cockpit and closed the door. Codie's hands held tight to the chair arms.

★ ★ ★

Inside the cockpit, Sam yanked off his tie and pulled his sweater up over his head, tossing it to the floor. He tapped Jim on the shoulder. "Move over, pal. I'll take it from here. Go stay with Codie. Pete, ride shotgun."

Sam folded his long frame into the seat and quickly clamped on the headset. "Tell me what you've got."

"Unsafe gear light's on."

"Emergency extension procedure?"

"Nothing works. Not even manual. I told the tower we might be in trouble."

"Okay. Let's pass over and let them take a look."

Radioing their intentions, Sam brought the plane in low over the tower.

"No gear, Golden Eagle," the tower radioed back.

"Then we have a first-class emergency here, Springfield."

"We're already foaming the runway. Crash trucks are standing by. How's your fuel? Do you need to burn it off?"

"No."

"Then come on in, Golden Eagle."

"That's easy for you to say."

Sam made the approach to the runway. He held the plane steady, begging the wings to stay level. He put his sights on the white, foam-covered lane that waited for them.

Randall held his breath.

"Right wing's dipping," Pete said evenly.

"I'm holding. I'm holding."

"You got it, Sambo. Lay it down easy."

The runway rose up to meet them. The Golden Eagle hit belly first, the vibration passing through the plane like a godly shudder. The screech of metal against concrete announced contact.

"Keep 'er level, Sambo, keep 'er level."

"Doing my best, Pete."

Foam splayed out on each side of the plane as it rode on its belly toward the end of the runway.

"We're running out of room, Sambo."

"I'm giving it all the brake I can. Any more and we cartwheel."

Golden Eagle tracked the centre line, groaning under the stress. A high, metal fence marked the end of the runway. The stop was sudden, just short of the fence.

Sam yanked off his headset and lowered his head. He rubbed a hand across his eyes. Sweat ran down his back, causing his shirt to cling in wet irritation. He unbuttoned the cuffs and rolled up the sleeves.

Randall turned in his seat to face him. "We're down, Sambo," he said hoarsely.

"Yeah, we're down. I owe you one." He put his hands against the arms of the seat and pushed himself up. Pulling open the cockpit door, he rushed to where Codie sat, her hands covering her face, her slender body trembling.

Sam gripped each of Codie's wrists and slowly, gently, lowered her hands. Relief and fear fought for a place in her eyes. He would never forgive himself for having put her life in such jeopardy.

"You all right?" he asked, unfastening her belt and pulling her up against him, straining to enclose her in his relief.

"Y — yes." She brought her arms about his neck, feeling his wet shirt, the heat of his tension. She buried her face in the musky curve of his shoulder. The trembling would not stop.

"Hang on to me, Codie," he said as they walked toward the front of the cabin. "Hang on tight."

Randall pulled back the hatch and stepped aside to allow Sam and Codie to pass through. Sam put firm hands to her waist and lifted her through the opening into the arms of two men who stood below. As she was gently lowered to the ground, Sam jumped from the plane, followed closely by Randall and Jim.

"What happened, Everett?" questioned one of the ground crew as they slushed through the foam.

"The Eagle has a broken limb, that's

all," answered Sam. "But it will heal."

Codie glanced toward the terminal to see Jesse waiting in the doorway, wringing his hands. When he caught sight of them, he pushed through the door, his arms held wide in anxious welcome.

"Scared me to death," he finally muttered when all the hugging was done.

"Me, too, Jesse," admitted Sam. "What are you doing here?"

"Thought you might want a driver."

"How'd you know we were in trouble?"

"I've got my spies," Jesse chuckled.

"Well, let's get back to Miss Oldham's, what do you say?"

"Fine by me."

Jesse led them to the Jeep where he climbed in behind the wheel while Sam spoke briefly with Randall. Randall nodded and slapped Sam lightly on the arm. "I'll call you, Sambo, when it's finished."

Sam lifted Codie up into the seat

behind Jesse. He sat beside her, his long legs stretched forward.

"Okay, Jesse, take us home," he sighed, his arm coming around Codie to pull her close to him, to hold onto her still trembling body. "It's going to be all right, Codie," he soothed, "it's going to be all right."

★ ★ ★

Miss Oldham stood on the porch, wrapped in a faded chenille robe, her hair done up in pink curlers. When they stopped at the kerb, she ran toward them, her worn slippers slap-slapping on the sidewalk.

"Mercy, mercy," she fussed, "what a scare you gave us. Now you get down here right now and let me fix you some coffee. Codie, are you all right? What's the matter with you, Sam, flying a busted plane like that. I swear, I don't know what I'm going to do with the two of you."

Sam and Codie stepped from the

van, trying unsuccessfully to hide their amusement at Miss Oldham's anxious patter. Inside the Bed 'n' Breakfast she shooed them to the kitchen where she insisted they sit down while she served sandwiches and coffee. Neither of them was hungry, but they ate nevertheless, knowing that to refuse would only concern Miss Oldham further. Jesse sat quietly watching her putter back and forth between cabinet and table.

"You're goin' to wear yourself out, Bertha," he warned. "Now sit down. If anybody needs anything, I'll get it."

Beneath the table, Sam's hand sought Codie's. He held it tightly, rubbing his thumb along the soft skin. Codie returned his touch, wanting never to let go.

For a while Codie and Sam sat in silence, content to be there, comfortable in each other's presence.

"Can you forgive me, Codie?" Sam said at last, turning in his chair to face her.

"For what?"

"For nearly killing us all," he whispered as his hand gently smoothed her hair.

"If you will forgive me."

"I will . . . if you'll tell me what you've done."

She pushed her chair back and stood, wanting to put some distance between them. What she had to say was not going to come easy. "I made you take that plane up, Sam."

"Oh?" He tilted his chair and locked his fingers behind his head. "How did you do that?"

"You would never have taken Golden Eagle up in that condition, but you did it because you thought I would be angry with you." She paced the length of the kitchen, her hands fluttering aimlessly. "I am responsible for what happened, Sam. I deserve whatever you feel right now. It's my fault the Golden Eagle went down."

19

SAM came forward in his chair and stood, his feet wide-spread, a scowl marring his forehead.

"Whoa, now, what are you saying?"

"I'm saying, if it hadn't been for me, you would never have insisted on taking off. Not with a busted landing gear."

His chuckle started deep inside him, rising to bring bright bluegreen sparkle to his eyes. "Oh, Codie, darling Codie. Come here." He opened his arms, his hands motioning for her to enter into their eagerness. Codie stood with her hands locked behind her back, a faint smile working at the corners of her mouth.

"You mean I'm forgiven?" she asked in a husky whisper.

"You are forgiven. Now, come here." His voice was low, insistent. Codie closed the distance between them, stepping into his arms, welcoming their confident command.

She held to him, not hearing the soft swish of the door as it opened.

"What's going on?" came a voice slurred with sleep.

Codie stepped from Sam's embrace just as Richard pushed the door all the way back. He stood staring at them, eyes squinting against the light.

"Codie? What are you doing up at this hour?" He held his hands clenched at his sides.

Sam stepped forward. "Nothing to worry about, Richard. We had a bit of trouble in the air, that's all."

"I see. Where've you been, Codie?"

"Hold it, Arlan," Sam spoke with a sharp, cutting edge. "Where Codie has been is none . . . "

Codie placed her hand on Sam's arm. "It's okay, Sam. Let me talk to him."

Sam looked at her over his shoulder, his body still turned toward Richard.

"Please, Sam," begged Codie.

He walked past Richard and pushed through the door. The only sound was the door slapping back into place. Codie motioned toward the table.

"Please, Richard, sit down."

His fists opened and closed, but he didn't move. "Where've you been, Codie?"

"Dallas."

"What for?"

"Dinner."

"I see. Must be nice to pick up and fly anywhere in the world. Must be nice."

"Richard, please, can't we talk about this rationally?"

"What's to be said? The cowboy won." He reached for the door. "I love you, Codie, but I'm no fool. Good-night."

"Good-night, Richard," she spoke to the closing door. "I'm sorry."

She stood for a moment, wishing for a way to ease Richard's pain. But there was none. She knew now why she had not been able to give Richard an answer. She loved him. As a friend.

But that was not enough. She was not in love with him.

She went to find Sam.

He sat on the front porch, leaning against the post, one knee raised to support his arm. At the sound of the door, he looked up through veiled eyes.

"Where's Richard?" he asked.

"Upstairs."

"What did he say?"

"He said 'the cowboy won'."

Sam stood with his back to her and descended the steps. Slowly he turned, his hands resting on his hips.

"Have I?" he asked.

"Yes," she answered.

He reached for her, gripping her by the waist to swing her down to him, to close her in his arms, to touch his lips to the softness of her neck.

"I love you, Codie Merideth. And I need you. I need you more than I have ever needed anyone or anything. Now," he sighed heavily, "will you please marry me so I can get my life back in order?"

"What's wrong with your life?" she whispered.

"Nothing now. Not a thing." He put her down and held her at arm's length. "Well?"

"Yes, I will marry you, Mr Everett, if you promise me one thing."

"Anything! What?"

"Promise me you'll never fly again . . . "

"What?"

" . . . unless the Eagle is ready."

"And if we get held over in Dallas, or Chicago, or . . . "

"I guess we'll just have to stay, won't we?"

"I guess we will." He put an arm around her waist and led her up the steps to the door of Miss Oldham's Bed 'n' Breakfast.

★ ★ ★

The next morning a package arrived for Sam by express mail. He ran up to Codie's room and pounded on the door.

"Codie! Codie?"

Pulling the sash of her peignoir around her waist, she turned the knob.

"Sam!" she scolded, "it's early. Why are you waking me at this hour?"

He held out the package.

"Open it," he smiled.

She took it from him and laid it on the bed. Slipping off the heavy cord, she folded back the brown paper. Inside was the plush terry towel, 'Nebraska' emblazoned across its wide surface. She lifted it and pressed it to her cheek.

"Now promise," Sam said as he leaned lazily against the doorframe, tugging at his earlobe, "promise me you won't leave it behind next time."

"I promise."

"I thought we'd go to Omaha for our honeymoon."

"Omaha?" she giggled. "What's in Omaha?"

"A plush hotel with room service.

Interested?" His tone was low and hoarse, rasping across his passion.

She walked to him, slipping willingly into his embrace as he held out his arm to receive her.

"Very interested," she whispered against the warm pulsing feel of his neck. "Very interested."

"Good. Now, get dressed. We're going for a ride."

"But, Sam I haven't eaten. I'm starved."

"So, we'll grab something on the way. Now, scoot, time's a-wastin'."

She laughed at his affected drawl as she closed the door and began dressing.

Sam was waiting for her in Jesse's Jeep when she came downstairs a few minutes later. He tapped his fingers on the steering wheel in exaggerated impatience. She smiled and climbed in beside him. When she was settled, he steered the Jeep away from the kerb with one hand as, with the other, he offered her a worn shoe box with a heavy string tied around its middle.

"What's this?" she asked.

"Breakfast."

Codie untied the string and lifted one corner of the lid. A warm, mouth-watering aroma wafted upward, causing her to close her eyes and sniff appreciatively. She pulled the lid off and reached inside for a fluffy, hot biscuit, a large sausage patty sandwiched between its buttery sides.

"Miss Oldham?" she managed between mouthfuls.

"Who else? There's a thermos of coffee on the back seat."

Codie twisted around in her seat to retrieve the container. She poured the steaming dark liquid into two styrofoam cups and handed one to Sam. He sipped it cautiously as he drove.

When she had finished eating, she wiped her hands on one of the napkins Miss Oldham had provided and stuffed it into her now empty cup. "Where are we going?" she asked.

"You'll see."

Codie studied the road ahead. They were on the highway that led out to the dam, the one that would pass the old building on the hill that Codie had coveted so for her big dream. She watched for the bright orange 'For Sale' sign as they rounded the last curve. Her heart jumped, anticipating the sight of it. Then, as if she had been slapped by a giant hand, she gasped.

Slashed across the six-foot high sign — in bold, red letters — was the word 'Sold'. Codie looked away quickly, wanting to shake the vision from her mind. Forget it, Codie, forget it.

You have more important things to think about now.

At the next intersection, Sam turned the Jeep around and headed back the way they had come.

"That's it?" she teased. "That's our ride?"

"Yep, that's it," he drawled. Then, with a suddenness that caused Codie to grab the dashboard for support, he pulled off the road onto the shoulder.

She frowned at him. "Do you have a death wish, Mr Everett? You could kill us both, stopping like that."

He turned to face her, his back against the door. "Come here," he whispered, motioning with his hand. She slid across the seat and leaned into his body, feeling the pounding of his heart as she laid her head on his chest. He put his hands on her shoulders and turned her around to face away from him.

"Look up there," he said.

Codie raised her eyes. There on the hill, the sunlight washing its magnificent bulk, was 'her' building. She swallowed against the disappointment that seemed to be stifling her very breath.

"Yes, I know," she murmured. "It was a great idea — once."

She could feel his breathing beneath her, smell the sweet, clean fragrance of his body. His arms wrapped her in a firm, all-encompassing love.

"It's still a good idea," he whispered.

"Apparently not. Look — 'Sold'.

Someone beat us to it."

He stirred ever so slightly. Codie heard the rustle as he pulled a folded paper from his pocket. He flipped it sharply to unfold it. "Take a look at this," he said.

She took the paper and held it at arm's length. It had an austere, official look about it. Codie glanced at the heading. She caught only one word before her eyes filled with tears. She could not read any further.

"Oh, Sam. Oh, Sam," she said huskily.

"It's yours, Sweetheart. You can have your dream, your home for children who need love. And you can have all the children you can manage. We'll hire a staff to help you and bring in some horses and a few chickens. We'll put in a pool and maybe some tennis courts. What do you think?"

"I think," she said as she twisted around to face him, "I think I love you more than any woman has ever loved any man anywhere." She touched her fingers to his cheek and drank in the sparkling goodness in his sea-deep blue eyes.

"Oh!" she gasped suddenly and pushed herself upright. "Oh, my, we can't."

"What do you mean, we can't? Of course, we can. It's all ours."

"But, Sam, what about your jets? You can't leave that. You can't give up Golden Eagle."

She felt rather than heard his deep chuckle. "Hold on, Codie. I'm not giving up Golden Eagle or any of my silver birds. I've already found a spot between here and Springfield. We're going to build our own runway and hangars. There is more than enough demand for charter service in this part of the country to keep us going for a long, long time."

She slipped back into his embrace, snuggling against him in complete surrender. The sun spilled its rays over the Loving Home, Codie's dream, sitting on the side of the hill.

WITH SOMEBODY ELSE
Theresa Charles

Rosamond sets off for Cornwall with Hugo to meet his family, blissfully unaware of the shocks in store for her.

A SUMMER FOR STRANGERS
Claire Hamilton

Because she had lost her job, her flat and she had no money, Tabitha agreed to pose as Adam's future wife although she believed the scheme to be deceitful and cruel.

VILLA OF SINGING WATER
Angela Petron

The disquieting incidents that occurred at the Vatican and the Colosseum did not trouble Jan at first, but then they became increasingly unpleasant and alarming.

DOCTOR NAPIER'S NURSE
Pauline Ash

When cousins Midge and Derry are entered as probationer nurses on the same day but at different hospitals they agree to exchange identities.

A GIRL LIKE JULIE
Louise Ellis

Caroline absolutely adored Hugh Barrington, but then Julie Crane came into their lives. Julie was the kind of girl who attracts men without even trying.

COUNTRY DOCTOR
Paula Lindsay

When Evan Richmond bought a practice in a remote country village he did not realise that a casual encounter would lead to the loss of his heart.

ENCORE
Helga Moray

Craig and Janet realise that their true happiness lies with each other, but it is only under traumatic circumstances that they can be reunited.

NICOLETTE
Ivy Preston

When Grant Alston came back into her life, Nicolette was faced with a dilemma. Should she follow the path of duty or the path of love?

THE GOLDEN PUMA
Margaret Way

Catherine's time was spent looking after her father's Queensland farm. But what life was there without David, who wasn't interested in her?

HOSPITAL BY THE LAKE
Anne Durham

Nurse Marguerite Ingleby was always ready to become personally involved with her patients, to the despair of Brian Field, the Senior Surgical Registrar, who loved her.

VALLEY OF CONFLICT
David Farrell

Isolated in a hostel in the French Alps, Ann Russell sees her fiancé being seduced by a young girl. Then comes the avalanche that imperils their lives.

NURSE'S CHOICE
Peggy Gaddis

A proposal of marriage from the incredibly handsome and wealthy Reagan was enough to upset any girl — and Brooke Martin was no exception.

A DANGEROUS MAN
Anne Goring

Photographer Polly Burton was on safari in Mombasa when she met enigmatic Leon Hammond. But unpredictability was the name of the game where Leon was concerned.

PRECIOUS INHERITANCE
Joan Moules

Karen's new life working for an authoress took her from Sussex to a foreign airstrip and a kidnapping; to a real life adventure as gripping as any in the books she typed.

VISION OF LOVE
Grace Richmond

When Kathy takes over the rundown country kennels she finds Alec Stinton, a local vet, very helpful. But their friendship arouses bitter jealousy and a tragedy seems inevitable.

CRUSADING NURSE
Jane Converse

It was handsome Dr. Corbett who opened Nurse Susan Leighton's eyes and who set her off on a lonely crusade against some powerful enemies and a shattering struggle against the man she loved.

WILD ENCHANTMENT
Christina Green

Rowan's agreeable new boss had a dream of creating a famous perfume using her precious Silverstar, but Rowan's plans were very different.

DESERT ROMANCE
Irene Ord

Sally agrees to take her sister Pam's place as La Chartreuse the dancer, but she finds out there is more to it than dyeing her hair red and looking like her sister.

HEART OF ICE
Marie Sidney

How was January to know that not only would the warmth of the Swiss people thaw out her frozen heart, but that she too would play her part in helping someone to live again?

LUCKY IN LOVE
Margaret Wood

Companion-secretary to wealthy gambler Laura Duxford, who lived in Monaco, seemed to Melanie a fabulous job. Especially as Melanie had already lost her heart to Laura's son, Julian.

NURSE TO PRINCESS JASMINE
Lilian Woodward

Nick's surgeon brother, Tom, performs an operation on an Arabian princess, and she invites Tom, Nick and his fiancé to Omander, where a web of deceit and intrigue closes about them.

THE WAYWARD HEART
Eileen Barry

Disaster-prone Katherine's nickname was "Kate Calamity", but her boss went too far with an outrageous proposal, which because of her latest disaster, she could not refuse.

FOUR WEEKS IN WINTER
Jane Donnelly

Tessa wasn't looking forward to meeting Paul Mellor again — she had made a fool of herself over him once before. But was Orme Jared's solution to her problem likely to be the right one?

SURGERY BY THE SEA
Sheila Douglas

Medical student Meg hadn't really wanted to go and work with a G.P. on the Welsh coast although the job had its compensations. But Owen Roberts was certainly not one of them!

HEAVEN IS HIGH
Anne Hampson

The new heir to the Manor of Marbeck had been found. But it was rather unfortunate that when he arrived unexpectedly he found an uninvited guest, complete with stetson and high boots.

LOVE WILL COME
Sarah Devon

June Baker's boss was not really her idea of her ideal man, but when she went from third typist to boss's secretary overnight she began to change her mind.

ESCAPE TO ROMANCE
Kay Winchester

Oliver and Jean first met on Swale Island. They were both trying to begin their lives afresh, but neither had bargained for complications from the past.